THE POLITICS
OF LOVE

By the Author

Jamis Bachman, Ghost Hunter

The Politics of Love

THE POLITICS OF LOVE

by
Jen Jensen

2020

THE POLITICS OF LOVE
© 2020 BY JEN JENSEN. ALL RIGHTS RESERVED.

ISBN 13: 978-1-63555-693-3

THIS TRADE PAPERBACK ORIGINAL IS PUBLISHED BY
BOLD STROKES BOOKS, INC.
P.O. BOX 249
VALLEY FALLS, NY 12185

FIRST EDITION: JULY 2020

CREDITS
EDITOR: CINDY CRESAP
PRODUCTION DESIGN: SUSAN RAMUNDO
COVER DESIGN BY JEANINE HENNING

Acknowledgments

I'm a Democrat, before anyone wonders. But I've spent a lot of time since 2016 trying to understand and humanize those folks with whom I don't agree. I like to think this book is a result of that effort.

I live in Arizona, a Red state turning Purple, more Libertarian than anything. It was easy to seek out Republicans like Shelley to talk with about these things. They supported gay marriage and didn't really care about people using the bathroom. They just wanted to preserve their freedom and personal liberty, without overbearing government systems getting in their way. They also wanted to keep their property taxes low and empower small businesses. They believed the market was the best way to equalize society. Their concerns seemed reasonable, and some of the animosity I felt, as a gay person, of Republican and conservative ideals, fell away. There are moderate, LGBTQ+ friendly Republicans out there. I found them. They're real and are not my adversary.

It's my hope that we can find a healthy way to debate the role of government in our lives, while we evolve as a species. Many thanks to everyone whose perspectives helped me evolve the last few years.

Dedication

For Sarah, my Democratic Socialist. I totally used each new chapter in this book to woo you. I'm glad it worked.

CHAPTER ONE

The cabs pressed through the intersection at Seventh Avenue in Manhattan, spots of yellow against dark cement and asphalt. Water from the rainstorm earlier in the day sprayed from beneath their tires, and the sounds of horns carried up to the open eatery. Shelley watched them through the window of Whole Foods.

She cut a piece of tofu with her fork and moved it to her lips. She focused on swallowing, folded her hands in her lap, and pressed her fingertips together. A bus stopped in the middle of the intersection, a police officer at the open door, likely telling the driver to move out of the notorious box, which should not be blocked but always was.

Shelley evened her breathing as the drama unfolded below and beat back the relentless waves of anxiety that plagued her every moment. She relaxed her hands and took a bite. The cop in the street below waved frantically at cars ahead of the bus to pull forward. They inched forward, one by one, as the light changed from red to green, again and again.

The situation was as stuck as she was.

The television on the wall was tuned to MSNBC. Andrea Mitchell discussed the ties between Trump and Russia. Her family celebrated Trump's election, but she had a queasy sensation in her stomach at the thought of him, as if America had sunk to the lowest common denominator in its reaction to change.

Being conservative was fine, as she was, but Trump was something entirely different. Populism meets subconscious racism and xenophobia, wrapped in MAGA, touted as nationalism. Shelley thought it was all a severe reaction to globalization, social media, and the previously unprecedented clash of human tribes.

She finished her food and tossed the container into the recycle bin. A table of adults, close to her age, pointed at her. She acknowledged them, uncertain of the attention she was about to receive, if not resigned to it. At the end of the table, a man said, "How does it feel to be such a bigot?"

Shelley ignored him, head down, pace a bit quicker. A woman next to him asked, "Closet case. Maybe you wouldn't hate gays so much if you got your pipes cleaned."

The rest of the words faded as the elevator doors closed. Her face burned. This direct engagement had begun after Trump was elected. For years, she'd toiled quietly behind the scenes of the Republican Party, operating on behalf of her father's organization, the American Religious Freedom Council. She consulted for the Republican National Party, CPEC, and every major conservative group in Washington, DC.

But the Left had never been as confrontational, and it was difficult to travel anywhere in Blue metropolitan areas without such an incident.

The stainless steel of the elevator doors reflected her image back, distorted by the imperfections of the metal and the scratches from the doors opening and closing. She tucked a stray piece of hair behind her ear and held her bag with both arms against her torso. Her high heels looked like blobs of black, and she felt hundreds of pounds overweight rather than forty. She tore her gaze away, uncomfortable. Shelley never paused to really look at herself. The lights on the elevator panel blinked as it moved down three floors.

The elevator lurched as it hit the ground floor, and she startled. She was so sensitive, the world's natural sensory outputs consumed her. The doors opened. She tucked her feelings of overwhelm inside, like a folder handkerchief, and marched forward as though she had all of herself, and the world, completely in control.

The checkout lines were busy. She negotiated her way to the front door through a sea of people. Outside, the damp fall air settled heavily on her shoulders. She pulled her slender, feminine bag closer and felt it hit her leg, a soft thud, repetitive and calming. She counted each connection, focused her breathing and thoughts on only that, and felt her heart rate slow, her hands loosen.

Shelley had done this since she was a child. For three years as an adolescent, she counted every step she took, and wrote the summation of them in her diary every night. "*Wednesday, April 21,1993 = 11,498 steps. Sunday, June 9,1996 = 13,500 steps.*" She employed pedometer methodology ahead of her time to self-correct crippling anxiety. Her therapist told her it was her earliest self-soothing tool.

Shelley couldn't remember when she stopped counting her steps, but thought it was sometime in high school when she became involved in student government and began to date

Tony. Shelley counted, falling into the familiar rhythm of the activity. She'd not thought about Tony for years, but there he was, fully formed in her mind's eye, as she walked up Seventh Avenue in Manhattan, on her way to MSNBC. She knew Tony lived in Manhattan because he'd tried to keep in touch with her after he left. She wanted to remain in contact with him but found it too difficult because her voice was caught somewhere under her throat and the space inside her chest cavity near her heartbeat.

When they were seniors, he told her he couldn't date her anymore because he was gay, and he thought maybe she was too. She'd never shared that secret with anyone, never dared, but recently, it had begun to bother her, a recurring thought wrestled back into place, only to greet her again and again. Shelley thought about finding Tony on Facebook and then felt her optimism recoil. It was something she did often. After thinking about extending herself, considering that someone might want contact with her, Shelley pulled the extraverted feeling back inside, tucked it away, and closed the lid on it.

She stopped at a crosswalk, pressed between thirty or more people, no idea where she was walking. The wind blew through the buildings, and the air was neither hot nor cold, just an uncomfortable wet in between. She shook out of her suit jacket and tucked it over her arm.

She searched MSNBC in Google Maps from her current location and opted to flag a cab. It was a mystery how she'd ended up where she was. She'd simply left her hotel room at nine and began to walk, enjoying the freedom of Manhattan streets. Skyscrapers. Cement. Hidden gardens and window flower boxes. Cops, pedestrians, crammed shopping centers, and Duane Reed pharmacies stuck under apartments in brick buildings, completely out of place. Scaffolding everywhere, the city under constant repair.

She slipped her jacket back on, stuck between hot and cold. The weather in Manhattan in late May was a confusing mix of warm and cool, wet and windy.

Shelley pushed through pedestrians and waved her arm at a passing cab. Tires squealed when he hit his brakes. She opened the back door, slid in, and said, "Thirty Rock please. Fastest route." The cab driver yanked the car into oncoming traffic. Shelley gripped the handle above the back window with one hand as the car lurched and rolled down the window with the other. The air smacked her face, wet and heavy. But it was better than the stuffy smell of the cab. She couldn't imagine the microorganisms on the seat and door handle. She took antibacterial sanitizer from her bag and rubbed her hands together when it seemed safe to let go.

How many thuds had she counted? She wasn't sure now, though she used to remember. The last number would sit behind the space between her eyes for ongoing review. Shelley read the driver's name on the taxi tag. She couldn't pronounce it so wouldn't try. Sometimes, she liked to thank people by their names, but wouldn't do it this time.

Charles Whitmore, her formidable, brilliant, Evangelical father, taught her to use people's names. He did it often, at church, charity events, grocery shopping, or standing in line at the bank. Shelley remembered riding to pick up Saturday night dinner from the pizza shop, watching him shake everyone's hands, use their names. He pulled her up to the side of him, hand on her shoulder. "Say hello to Sam, Shelley. He works hard at the lumber mill." He would continue, one after another, as people gathered around the lawyer turned pastor with a flock of thirty thousand people. He smiled at everyone he met, a trait she inherited, even if her smile was slower to emerge. She also inherited his large brown eyes, fastidiousness, and mind.

The cab driver jammed on the brakes, and Shelley rocked violently in the back seat and smacked against the seat. He made eye contact with her and yelled, "Sorry, sit back." She scooted to the back of the seat. These trips to the city excited her. She marked the days between visits on her iPhone calendar. The energy of the city was so different from anything she'd known before, it jolted her, like the pleasant but disconcerting shock of seeing someone she knew in a distant airport.

The cab jerked. Thirty Rock was visible. Shelley waved at the driver.

"Here is fine," she said. He slammed the brakes and hit the button to end the fare. Shelley handed him thirty dollars and waved for him to keep the balance. He took the money, obviously unimpressed with the tip. She held her bag in her arms. The wind was strong against her steps, like it wanted to keep her from MSNBC.

Her father supported her visits to the news show. The format allowed for discussion and debate, and she was typically paired with a liberal to provide a counterpoint perspective, given the polarization of American news. The MSNBC producer who hired her said they found her the least offensive of southern conservatives. She'd not relayed that to her father.

She traveled to Manhattan twice a month for a day, but in the last four months she extended her time by a day on either side. She'd taken the time to read, write, and explore, free of the weight and burden of her birthright. The guards recognized her as a regular and waved her ahead of the line. The metal detectors were silent as she stepped through them. She thanked them politely and moved toward the elevators. She rushed into one just as the doors began to close, and stumbled into another female.

"Whoa there," she said with a smile. "You about took both of us out." She adjusted a backpack held loosely over one shoulder.

"I think my heel got caught in the groove there." Shelley straightened her posture, felt flustered, and held out her hand. "Shelley Whitmore. Thank you for catching me."

The woman looked at her outstretched hand, then met her eyes. "I know who you are." She held her eye contact and lifted her hand. "Rand Thomas." Shelley registered who stood before her and felt a grating sensation gnaw at her center. The feeling emerged during different times in her life, in different cycles, but it always left her slightly off balance. In recent years, it made her feel a sense of vertigo, and sometimes the world spun, as it did in the elevator holding Rand's hand.

Rand withdrew against the railing where it angled at the back of the elevator. Shelley drew a tight breath and looked down at her feet. It was her reaction to meeting new people, and particularly, people who might see through her. Shelley retreated, and a deep shame she wasn't able to articulate rose to hold her words hostage.

Rand spoke to break the awkward silence. "I won't bite." The elevator chimed as they passed a floor.

Shelley met Rand's kind eyes, noted their gray-green color, the sharp angle of her jaw, her short, messy hair, and the perfect proportion of her nose between two manicured eyebrows. Shelley's face burned again. "I didn't think you would."

"But you don't want to talk anymore?"

"It's not that. I was just waiting, I think," Shelley said.

Rand inclined her strong jaw up, urging her to continue. When Shelley didn't, Rand said, "Waiting for what?"

Shelley jerked her eyes up from the tile of the elevator, noting sixteen separate tiles, and three cracks which spread across seven. "Your derision. Judgment."

"Should I feel sorry for you? Or the twelve-year-old who hears what your father has to say and would rather kill themselves than live openly and well as a queer person?" The doors chimed open, grating, and there were tears behind Shelley's eyes she wouldn't let fall, mistress of the stymied emotion. "See you on the show." Rand stepped from the elevator first, and Shelley watched her walk away and almost missed getting off the elevator before the doors closed.

Shelley's heel slipped into the crack again, but she steadied herself. Rand had said her father, not her, and she yanked hold of herself, somewhere deep inside, near her center, and regained composure. She and her father were separate people, and this thought lingered in the front of her consciousness.

She moved the same direction Rand did. Her hair and makeup needed attention before she went on the air.

CHAPTER TWO

W e're here with Rand Thomas, therapist, writer, activist and Shelley Whitmore, attorney, political consultant, and writer." Greg Jackson, afternoon host of the daily news, turned to face them. "We appreciate you both being here today." Both smiled politely, waiting. "We're here to talk about transgender bathroom access in schools, universities, and public spaces."

The camera swung wide to capture all three of them in view. Shelley's back was straight, hands folded, hair pulled tight in a bun, tapered at the base of her head. She looked reserved and educated, almost a caricature of a conservative lawyer. Rand sat with an arm casually on the table, at an angle so she could see Greg, Shelley, and the camera. She wore a gray button-down shirt with dark jeans and casual shoes. Greg wore a three-piece suit with a tie and continued.

"We've seen a huge uptake in these transgender bills, only allowing people to access them based on their biological sex. The left claims this is transphobic and prohibitive. The right claims it is necessary to protect women from predatory men. We don't need to go into a ton of detail about all the different bills, in multiple red states, or the counter-bills in blue states, but if our viewers want to review it, they can visit our blog today. We've posted in-depth analysis of all of them. Generally, what we want to do with Rand and Shelley is talk about this conceptually and philosophically. Rand, do you want to begin?"

"Thanks, Greg. I'm not sure this is really a philosophical issue. I think people just have to pee." Greg laughed, but Shelley was impassive and watched Rand as she spoke. "What shocks me about these bills is that they're not really about transgender people. They're about dangerous, predatory men. Think about it like this—if you were to use the bathroom next to a real, live transgender person you probably wouldn't know. That's what really gets to people, I think. With surgery and hormones, transgender people can amend their outer selves to align with their inner vision of themselves and no one knows any different. What scares people is this fear that creepy, predatory men who prey on women and children will take advantage of bathroom access. I think this calls for America to examine their perception of men."

"That's an interesting take on it, Rand," Greg said.

"Listen, I have the hardest time peeing in public because I'm so butch." Shelley gasped and Rand held eye contact with her. "People run after me, chase me into public bathrooms. 'That's the women's bathroom,' they scream, like I'm committing murder. I've addressed these incidents as positively as possible, but I can tell you they've happened more and more often since these bills cropped up. It's irrational fearmongering."

"I can't even imagine," Greg said. Shelley was quiet.

"We're afraid of gender nonconforming people like me. We're afraid of transgender people. But mostly, we're afraid of men. I think we need to repair masculinity."

"I sometimes forget you're a therapist first," Greg said.

"After the show we can explore your childhood issues."

"Tell me it's a flat rate and you won't bill by the hour," Greg said. "Seriously, though, what's the answer?"

"There is no need to be afraid of transgender people. It might make you feel uncomfortable, but embrace that, don't run from it, and try to understand why. Different can be scary when you don't understand. If you're out there and you feel that way, maybe it might help to go to YouTube and watch videos about transgender kids and adults. I'll give Greg some links to put up on the website," Rand said.

"I didn't mean to take over. Shelley and I met in the elevator, where I saved her from an unfortunate heel accident." Rand paused. "Her heels, not mine." Greg laughed again. "We don't need to talk about it. It was gruesome, but we both made it out alive."

Shelley met her eyes and smiled, and heat spread across her cheeks.

"I'm glad everything worked out okay," Greg said.

"It did," Rand said.

Shelley looked down at the microphone inside her shirt, then at Greg. She had all the appropriate talking points aligned in her head. A minority shouldn't be able to make the majority feel uncomfortable to accommodate their every whim. The Judeo-Christian ethic built Western civilization. No culture accepted the idea of gender swapping, a severe psychological dysfunction that required medical, psychological, and spiritual help. But nothing came out. None of the words felt right. She'd prefer to be on the show and talk about public spending, taxes, individual liberty, personal responsibility, and social mobility.

Instead of what she was supposed to say, Shelley said, "I think I need to watch some YouTube videos."

Greg choked on his coffee. Shelley made eye contact with Rand, and then stared at her own hands. The production team was silent. "Shelley, are you serious? Or are you placating Rand?"

"I don't speak for all of the Right. What Rand said really hit me. I personally have no attachment to transgender bathroom bills. Over-regulation of people's private lives is an intrusion of government, and I favor small government. I don't think the state has a vested interest in limiting gender expression or prohibiting transition, thusly, I can't justify an argument against access. The concern doesn't add up. It's not rational," Shelley said, focused in thought, eyes fixed on a spot above Greg's shoulder.

"When you think it through, break it down, it doesn't really matter. Even if people object on religious grounds to transition, we don't live in a religious theocracy where the will of one religion is imposed. It is only tolerated in spaces where we have to protect personal liberty. So, if you're religious and don't believe it's moral to transition, then don't. But it's not in the state's interest to limit the rights and access for others who are not."

"You sound Libertarian," Rand said. "Like a real one."

"I apologize. We should probably screen topics better," Shelley said. She laughed and felt a lightness of being she'd not felt before, mind made up on her own, a momentary glimpse of freedom at the desk by Rand's side, the cameras pointed her way.

"I'm just so shocked," Greg exclaimed.

"I could offer point by point the perspective of the folks championing these bills, and Rand could refute them one by one, if you'd like." Then there was a wave of panic. What would her family do and say when she returned home?

Greg turned to the camera. "We'll be right back to do just that after this commercial break."

The cameras stopped recording and Rand turned to Shelley, who held perfectly still, eyes fixed on her hands in front of her. There were red splotches on her skin above and between her breasts. She hated her body's nervous responses.

"Why did you do that?" It was Rand. Greg talked with a production assistant, telling them to get the clip up online immediately.

Shelley gathered her breath and turned to meet Rand's eyes. "Because you're right and I'm tired of fighting about things that don't matter." Then, with a rush, "Of course it matters to transgender people, I don't mean that."

Rand placed her hand on her arm before withdrawing to her own space. "It's okay. I understand. Thank you." The spot on her arm Rand touched was still warm though she knew rationally that wasn't possible.

Shelley was pleased to have received her gratitude, oddly eager for more. The show resumed with the conversation, and by the time they were finished, the video of her conceding to Rand was traveling the digital networks. Shelley Whitmore made breaking news as the first hard-right Christian Evangelical to support transgender people's rights. She didn't think about any of this, or what it would mean when she returned home, because she was too focused on pretending not to notice the length of Rand's fingers as she pointed at the desk to outline her ideas, and the heat of her body to the left of her, close enough to touch if she were brave enough. But she wasn't. She'd done enough for the day.

CHAPTER THREE

Shelley replaced her skirt and heels with jeans and tennis shoes. Her duty done at MSNBC, she intended to resume walking around the city. Shelley looked forward to a quiet dinner in a village restaurant, her options for vegan food endless in Manhattan. Slipping into her jeans was a relief, and she sat on the small sofa in the dressing room to tie her shoes. Still sitting, she slipped off her jacket and sleeveless shirt and pulled on a light thermal.

Shelley shook her hair free and fixed it in a loose braid on the back of her neck. She took contacts from her eyes, slipped them into their case, and put heavy dark plastic glasses on. Her vision sharpened and she pushed the glasses up her nose. Shelley opened the door, still looking in her purse, stepped, and heard, "Whoa! Are you after me?"

Rand was in the doorway, arms out, smiling. Shelley covered her mouth with her free hand, bag on her shoulder. "Oh my God. You need to take out an insurance policy if I'm anywhere near you."

"You look…" Rand said, thought trailing off.

"I changed," Shelley said, stating the obvious. Rand hadn't changed anything but the button-down shirt she'd been wearing. Now she wore a light blue, faded T-shirt and a green hoodie. "Is it bad?" Shelley asked, immediately regretting the question. It sounded insecure and needy. Likely, she thought with ire, because she was.

"No," Rand said. "Just different. More comfortable. I like your glasses." There were seven pictures on the wall behind Rand. "Listen, I wanted to apologize for earlier and to say thank you for today."

Shelley stopped counting. "You're welcome." Then she resumed counting to ten. "It's okay about earlier. I understand." She willed herself to look at Rand. "You said my dad, anyway. I know how he feels. I'm figuring out how I feel." Rand tipped her head, uncertain. "In the elevator," Shelley explained. "You said my dad, not me. That mattered."

Rand's expression changed, and Shelley met her eyes, found them kind, accepting, and wanted to cry. Shelley backed into the dressing room. "I was just leaving," she said, wondering about her choice to retreat.

"Yeah, me too. Are you busy? Do you want to get an early dinner with me?" Shelley did, and her heart leapt, but she controlled it, or hoped, as looking too eager was probably repellant. Or so she'd heard.

"I'd love to."

"Let's go. I heard you're vegan, which is still the least surprising thing I've learned about you today. I know a great place," Rand said. Shelley took three large steps, not wanting Rand to leave without her. They walked through the hall together, Shelley keeping pace with Rand's long strides. They stopped at the elevator and Rand punched the button. Rand was a few inches shorter than she was. She'd thought Rand was taller, but she supposed it was her confidence and gait.

Then she saw the ring on Rand's left ring finger and her heart slipped from its lofty perch and landed with a thud right in front of her feet. Shelley was sure she'd trip on it. Rand was married. She should have known that, but the truth was she only knew of her activism and work, nothing of her personal life. Before the elevator, she didn't even know what Rand looked like. Shelley wanted to excuse herself from dinner but was uncertain of the reason. Was she attracted to Rand? The answer was yes.

Tony had been right all those years ago. They were friends and he never pressured her for more. He filled the hours of her loneliness, and their chemistry made the world seem less barren and bleak. She'd known then but lacked the capacity to do anything about it. Shame spread through her like lava, decimating everything it touched. She was a mystery to herself, a stranger living inside her own body. Shelley counted the tiles on the wall between the two elevators.

Rand turned to her with a smile. "How long have you been vegan?" Shelley caught her breath. "Are you okay?" Shelley's mind raced. Not only was Rand beautiful, she was kind and intuitive too. Was beautiful the right word? "Shelley?"

"Oh, yeah, I'm fine," Shelley said. "I drifted away in thought. It happens."

The elevator doors finally opened. Rand waved her in first. "Flights of fancy?"

"Should see me with a good book," Shelley said.

"You like to read?"

"Love to," Shelley said eagerly, and then retreated again. She turned to face the elevator doors, aware of Rand. "What did you ask me?"

"I wondered how long you'd been vegan."

"Since I was sixteen," Shelley said.

"That's young." Shelley didn't volunteer anymore. "My wife was vegan." Shelley was curious. "She passed away. Three years ago." Instinctively, Shelley rested her hand on Rand's arm, waiting. "Mood bomb. Sorry." She smiled, lines around her eyes crinkling. Shelley looked at her with tenderness but pulled her hand back quickly.

"I'm sorry for your loss."

"Thank you. Exactly three years ago next week. Probably why it's top of mind. But we don't have to spend a lot of time on it. I don't mean to weigh us down. I'd like to talk more about what happened on the show, if you'd like."

Shelley did, and they walked, the late afternoon sun fading, the streets filling with pedestrians leaving jobs, rushing for subways and buses. Shelley was jostled by the throngs of crowds and lost sight of Rand after she was caught in a swell and swept into the middle of the road. Shelley didn't have Rand's phone number and panicked, but then there were warm fingers around her wrist and a tug. Rand pulled, arm around her waist.

"I hate New York City," Rand said, hauling Shelley to the open space on the sidewalk against the building. "Let's get a cab. Wait here?" Rand flagged down a cab, beckoned Shelley, and together they fled, momentarily relieved of the chaos.

❖

Shelley took the final bite of her vegan dahl makhani, cooked in coconut milk, ginger, and tomatoes and smiled at Rand, happier than she'd remembered being in her adult life.

She didn't quite know how to qualify that thought and share with Rand in a way that wouldn't make her seem desperate and strange, so tucked it away for later. The small restaurant was hidden on Bleecker, in a downstairs room below a bar, deep inside Greenwich Village. The noise above disappeared as they stepped down the stairs.

Their food came quickly, and they spent most of their time in casual conversation about the menu, food, and other restaurants. The brick walls were exposed, and metal frames hung from wires. Shelley assumed they were pictures of patrons, but she didn't ask. A small curtain separated the dining area from the kitchen, which didn't look very big, a common feature of NYC restaurants.

"I ate so fast," Shelley said with a shy smile.

"It was just one dish," Rand said. "Let's get some pakora?" Shelley motioned to the menu, which Rand tipped toward her. Shelley pointed to a dish. "Potatoes too. These have spinach." Shelley held up two thumbs in agreement. Rand waived to the server and placed the order.

"I'm food motivated." Shelley sipped her Diet Coke, laughing as she folded her napkin in her lap.

Rand had both elbows on the table. Shelley was drawn toward her and inched forward. What was she doing?

"Most vegans are, I think. If you can find food, you love to eat," Rand said. Shelley agreed, uncertain what else to say. "You're not who I thought you were. I spend all this time telling people not to have preconceived notions about who people are, and I do it too."

The tiles on the wall drew Shelley's attention, but she willed herself not to count. Instead, she met Rand's eyes. "It's not all unfair, your preconceived notions. I honestly don't know what I'm doing. Or why I'm doing it. It's like I went to sleep sometime in my teens when I should have individuated and just powered down. Lately, I don't know. Everything inside of me is changing."

"What's changing?"

"I don't know if I'm saying that right," Shelley said.

"It's not about saying it right or not. It's about saying what you feel. The answers can be conflicting and confusing."

"You sound like a therapist," Shelley said.

"Well." Rand pulled a face. "Sorry. You agreed to dinner. Not a session."

"No, it's fine. I'm just not sure how to answer. I don't know the answer, I guess."

"That's fair." Rand took a drink.

"I was wondering," Shelley said, uncertain, but plunged ahead. "Rand. Is that your real name?"

"Rand Thomas sounds fake," she said. "Miranda is my given name. By the time I was seven, I knew I was no Miranda. I woke my mom up one morning and asked to be called Rand. She and my father agreed, made the changes, and here I am."

"Your parents just agreed?"

"If I'd told them I wanted to be a boy, they'd have supported me. That didn't feel quite right either. I just didn't want to be Miranda. Everything else seemed acceptable. My parents are San Francisco leftists. My mom teaches English literature at Berkeley, and my father is a biochemist researcher."

"I can't imagine. You know who my parents are." Shelley tried to process the idea of a childhood so different from her own.

"I don't take my privilege for granted."

"Is it privilege?" Shelley questioned Rand earnestly.

"To be loved, accepted, supported, and included for exactly who you are, with no expectation of change? I think it's the best privilege there is." As an onslaught of confusing emotion erupted, Shelley momentarily lost her balance. Rand put her hand on her arm. Her struggle to restore calm must have been obvious. It embarrassed her. The warmth of Rand's hand traveled through her light thermal, and a tickle of desire unwound in her stomach, adding to the confusing pile of emotions Shelley was buried beneath.

"Shelley," Rand said, "whatever it is, when you're ready, if you need help, whatever—" The pressure of Rand's hand on her arm intensified before she released her grasp. "I can listen. Be your friend."

Shelley, normally a master at sublimation, struggled for recovery. "Thank you." She held Rand's eyes, and the server set down their food. Her friend. Was it normal to feel heat burn through the middle of you when a new friend touched you?

"Hate to interrupt a moment, ladies. But I've got your pakora," the server said.

Shelley forced a smile. "I might share this," she said, desperate to change to subject. She pushed a few pieces onto her plate. "Might."

CHAPTER FOUR

Rand waited on the sidewalk. The sun set as they ate, and now the city buzzed with nighttime electricity. The swarms of people were settled into apartments, trains to the boroughs, or tucked away in restaurants like the one from which she just stepped. Rand visited the city from time to time but was noticing more than normal. In a blinding moment of clarity, she realized it was likely because of Shelley. There was something innocent and youthful about her enjoyment of the city, a sort of hope Rand lost years before. At dinner, she discovered Shelley was almost a decade younger. Maybe it was that, Rand thought as Shelley came up the stairs.

Rand didn't want to leave her and greeted her with a smile, heart hammering. The emotion was new and surprising, the draw was undeniable. Shelley stopped in front of her and lifted her bag on her shoulder. "Are you busy?"

"No," Shelley said, eyes alive.

"Let's walk to Times Square. Can you believe I've never been?"

"Really? But my feet are tired. Let's take a cab," Shelley said. "My turn." Shelley moved to the curb, watching oncoming traffic.

Their hands brushed against each other. Rand thought about taking Shelley's hand. She was so distracted by the thought, Shelley's shout at a taxi startled her.

"Got one," Shelley said. Rand waited for Shelley to get in and slipped in next to her, sitting close enough that she felt Shelley's arm and thigh against her own.

Shelley didn't move away from her as she spoke to the driver. "Times Square, please."

He yanked the car into oncoming traffic and Rand slid closer to Shelley, reaching up to grab the handle above the door. "Hold on." Shelley laughed, as they were thrown across the back seat and the driver turned crazily into oncoming traffic. Rand turned, braced against Shelley's side.

"It's a bit like a roller coaster. Kind of fun," Rand said.

"I hate them. Went once, during high school. I was a victim of peer pressure," Shelley said. The driver slammed on the brakes. Rand put her arm around Shelley to brace them in the back seat.

Over Shelley's shoulder, on the street corner, a man held a white poster sign, *The earth is flat and the vortex is collapsing.*

Rand pointed and Shelley read it out loud as the taxi lurched forward. In that moment, Rand wanted nothing more than for Shelley to never stop reading things out loud. The combination of her southern accent and calm tone cascaded into Rand's senses like a Bach concerto on a dark, cold night, fireplace lit.

"What if he's right? I mean, seriously? We could be mocking him and he's the one with all the answers," Rand said.

"Do you think the earth is flat? That's critical information for me to know if we're going to socialize," Shelley joked, at ease.

Rand help up a hand and made a face. "I've never been to outer space, so—" The driver stopped at a light. "Is it more bizarre to believe a creator God made us? Then gave barely literate desert dwellers a set of arbitrary ancient laws to follow into infinity and beyond? Then, if we don't continue to listen, he lets us suffer and withholds love, condemning us to hell? All the while, keeping himself invisible in the world? And not adjusting any of the parameters of his rules for progress and understanding?"

"I take it you don't believe in God?"

"No. I don't. If God exists, he's a dick," Rand said. "If your God is real, he has a lot of explaining to do for all the evil and suffering in the world he created." Shelley listened, deep brown eyes intently fixed on Rand.

Rand held her gaze. How would it feel to just reach and touch her face? Pull her forward for a kiss?

"We're here," the driver said.

Shelley dug in her purse for money. Rand waved at her to stop, but she refused. They stood on the corner, the flashing lights of Times Square just around the corner. There was a charge in the air, and the hairs on Rand's arm stood up. Her heart hammered in her chest. The weight of her burdens and past were gone. Rand was lighter and freer than she'd been in so long the sensation shocked her. She studied Shelley. A light wind blew against her face and strands of hair danced in the air above her head.

Shelley stared at the lights, quiet, obviously away in thought. Rand touched her arm and Shelley smiled. "Are you worried the earth is really flat now?"

Shelley laughed and touched her shoulder with her own. It felt so natural it took Rand a few moments to notice it. They moved toward Times Square, shoulders touching, in stride with one another. As they turned the corner, the bright lights of Times Square startled Shelley and she closed her eyes. Rand saw it.

"Allow me to be chivalrous," Rand said, smiling, playful, and lifted Shelley's hand to hold the bend of her elbow. They walked together and paused to stare at flashing billboards, lights, and stores. Rand took pictures for a group of tourists. They stopped at an overwhelmed Starbucks for coffee.

They found a small bench in the middle of the square and huddled together and watched the crowds. Rand slipped her arm behind Shelley as she pointed at a solo guitarist playing on the corner. In momentary lulls of noise from the crowd, they could hear his music filter toward them. They sat on the bench for a while, the movement of life around them, with the haunting, vague strumming of guitar their companion.

Shelley's profile was striking in the bright, blinking lights of Times Square. Rand rubbed Shelley's shoulder with her thumb absentmindedly. Shelley turned to her as a guitar movement moved toward a crescendo. Rand leaned forward, legs down on the ground now. Shelley's nose was perfect, a strong, solid line, her other features symmetrical. Behind her thick glasses, dark brown eyes glinted simultaneously with brilliance and confusion.

Rand hadn't expected to think Shelley Whitmore was pretty, but she did. She could be gorgeous, but lacked confidence. She held her body stiffly, like she didn't know what to do with it. Her gestures were not casual, and she didn't move with ease. It was as if her body reflected the deep angst she carried inside. Watching her, bright blue and orange neon flickering behind her, was when Rand realized Shelley was gay. Rand looked at her with new understanding. A fresh wave of emotion erupted in her chest, and any hostility about political differences melted away with the surprising empathy that commandeered her body.

Rand wanted to kiss her there, in that moment, as the noise around them stilled and the lights played across her face. Rand was overcome by the sensation of Shelley next to her, panicked, and turned away, eyes closed. The music stopped.

Shelley shuddered and Rand pulled away. "Should we go? It's late."

There was disappointment on Shelley's face, but they walked together, arms brushing, both silent. Rand retreated from the intensity of the connection she'd just felt. It was too much to imagine that after all this time, she'd feel something for a closeted Republican. Shelley should be her arch-nemesis and she was thinking about how silky her hair would feel between her fingertips? She needed time to examine her feelings and motivation.

❖

As they arrived at the edge of Times Square, close to midnight, Shelley's steps were lighter than they were when she began her day, as if all of her were in the present moment. The energy of the city stirred her senses together and she felt a tangle of confusion, desire, and blind excitement standing next to Rand, who turned to look at her.

"I guess I should get back to my hotel," Rand said. Shelley thought there was a forlorn sound to it, but didn't dare press for clarity.

"My flight leaves at four a.m." Shelley looked at her watch.

"You'll barely sleep," Rand said. "Mine doesn't leave until afternoon."

"It's okay. I had such a great time. I've never done this."

"Me either," Rand said, holding Shelley's gaze. Shouts filtered up behind them from the busy streets. Rand turned to look, and then back to Shelley.

"Can we keep in touch?" Shelley asked and jammed her hands in her pockets, unsure what to do as they said good-bye.

"Of course," Rand answered.

"I'll give you my phone number and email address," Shelley said, holding her phone in both hands. On the dark corner of a Manhattan street, as a gust of wind swept toward them, Shelley and Rand huddled together, phones out, clarifying email addresses and numbers. When they finished, Shelley looked directly into Rand's eyes and smiled. Shelley hugged Rand.

Rand flinched, involuntarily, shocked, but upon feeling Shelley's arms around her neck, took a deep breath and surrendered into the moment. She wrapped her arms around Shelley's waist and closed her eyes. Shelley fit in her arms. Rand still let go before Shelley.

"I've had a great time," Rand said. Shelley lifted a hand up to fix the string on Rand's hoodie, but Rand jerked away and around her. "There's a cab." Rand waved her arm. "You go first," Rand said, opening the door. "I have more time."

Shelley looked at the open car door and back at Rand and shifted her bag on her shoulder. "I'll email you." Shelley seemed reluctant to leave but climbed in the cab. Rand closed the door. Shelley looked at her through the back window, raising her hand in good-bye. Rand did the same as the wind increased in its intensity and huge droplets of water began to fall. She raced under an awning as Shelley's taxi disappeared around the corner.

CHAPTER FIVE

Rand crossed her legs and looked at Mary from the corner of her eyes, facing the window. "Don't therapathize me."

"That's ridiculous and you know it," Mary said, voice calm. Rand waved her hand. "You're a terrible patient." Mary wore her dyed bright red hair in a short bob. Rand noticed her flowing, linen dress and thought she looked more like a fortune-teller than a therapist, and the sound of her bracelets when she moved her arm was distracting.

"I feel angry today. Angsty," Rand said. "I'm obviously also making up words."

"What does that say to you about how you feel?"

"Really?" Rand asked, shifting in her seat.

"Yes." Nothing else.

"I'm trying to create my own reality."

"That's actually quite insightful," Mary said. "Keep going."

"I'm making up words with you because I just want my life to be my own. I want it all to stop. I'm tired." There were tears in Rand's eyes.

"Okay," Mary said softly. "There we are. Let's go there."

"Kim's parents sued me. My dead wife's parents want to torture me. They believe I'm keeping some priceless family ring that belonged to a maternal grandmother three hundred years back. First, they wanted her childhood belongings. Remember their lawyer sent me a letter for that? I offered to let them come take whatever they wanted. Her mom refused to come in, said she wanted a police officer to come with her. After all that, they took five old storybooks because Kim kept nothing else. I sold the house we lived in. We both paid into it. I don't even know how I'd carve out her portion. I used her IRA to pay her medical bills. I donated her clothes to a women's shelter. Everything else we had was jointly acquired. I donated what I could and sold the furniture for pennies at a yard sale. I didn't want any of it. They think I'm hiding things, family heirlooms. It's even more awful because Kim had cut them off years before her death. She didn't even want me to invite them to her funeral, but I did. I had to."

"Remind me how many times this has come up?"

"It's been happening since Kim died." Rand rubbed her eyes. "I should just give them a chunk of money. Or maybe I'll sell everything, give the money to charity, and flee the country."

"Do you really want to do that?" Mary put her notebook down, content to listen.

"No," Rand said. "I don't. But..." Rand walked to the window.

"What?" Mary turned to face her, not moving from her chair.

"I feel like maybe it's some sort of punishment."

"For what, Rand?"

"For living when she's dead. For wanting to move on. This keeps me with her. I can't even take off the ring." Rand looked at her hand and spun the ring around her finger. She'd done that for the past three years. At night, she'd sit in bed with a book and work the ring slowly up her finger, to the knuckle, before pushing it back down. One night she took it off and set it on the nightstand. She slid down into the sheets and closed her eyes. Panic overwhelmed her and she grabbed for the ring.

She told Mary this as she stood by the window, the glaring hot summer sun scorching the earth outside. The glare from a car's mirror stung her eyes. Rand wondered why it was so unseasonably warm.

"Your guilt comes up a lot." Rand didn't say anything, so Mary continued. "Rand, don't let them win." Rand gave Mary a thumbs-up but said nothing else. "Rand."

"I know. Stop being my therapist for a minute."

"Okay," Mary said. She took off her glasses.

"We were friends before I started coming here."

"We were," Mary agreed. Rand sat back down. "Is that important?"

"I think so. I don't know why I said it." Mary shrugged, listening. Rand crossed her legs, looked behind her, then at the picture of dogs on a beach, playing. "I want a dog."

"Really? Connection. Family. That's what you're yearning for. Have you talked to your parents?"

"I called Mom last night when I got the letter. She wants to ask for help at the law school. She's urging me to seek out legal help from the justice system. She says it is harassment. She's livid. I told her not to make contact with them because it will just make it worse."

"Why don't you become more aggressive dealing with this, Rand?"

Rand sighed, hands in her lap. Kim filled her mind. She saw her as they were when they were thirteen, riding their bikes down to the bay, hands in the air as they dropped down hills. At eighteen when they left for college, and twenty-three when they finished graduate school. She saw their first apartment, car, and their small wedding as soon as it was legal. Then they were thirtysomething, working full time, lives settled, and they rarely touched.

They were the best of friends, but Rand wasn't in love with Kim and wondered if she'd ever been. The realization came in a benign moment, as far as those moments go. At the table, drinking coffee while she looked at the paper, Rand looked up at Kim as she buttered toast, and it occurred to her that her whole life had just happened.

The thought propelled her into a deep dive of self-discovery, therapy, and her first handful of sessions with Mary, who'd been a colleague and friend when she worked at the county hospital admitting psychiatric patients in the emergency room. Almost six months later, she was ready to tell Kim she wanted to move on, explore independent life, free them both to truly fall in love.

But when she'd gotten home, Kim sat ashen on the couch. She'd not felt well, her fatigue levels increasing with each passing day. Rand thought she was depressed. It was here, on the day Rand was to request a divorce, that Kim told her she had stage three ovarian cancer and it had spread to her brain, liver, and lungs.

Rand put her face in her hands. Mary leaned forward and touched her arm. "What is it?"

"I wanted to leave her. You know that."

"I did," Mary said.

"I feel like this is my fault. Guilty. Maybe I owe her parents."

"I don't need to tell you that's not rational. You've not admitted this before. Why now?"

"Because I want to leave her again. I just want to move on. I just want this to stop."

❖

The view from the window in Rand's office was Piestewa Peak. It was why she chose it. Her phone rang. "This is Rand."

"Hey, it's me." It was Jamie, her best friend. "I texted you. Didn't answer. Then I called your cell. Didn't answer. Had to call your landline. Wasn't sure the mobile phone could call a landline, because you're the only person I know who has one."

"I told you some of my patients have HIPAA concerns with mobile phones." Rand said mo-bile, emphasizing to make her point. Jamie laughed.

"Whatever. Weirdo. Want to come over for dinner? Rachel is off from the hospital at four and she's coming over." Rachel, her other best friend. They'd known each other since college at UCLA.

"Yeah. I'll be there. What time?"

"Anytime is fine. When you're done." Jamie hung up and Rand quietly tucked the phone back on the receiver. It wasn't weird she still had a landline. The message light blinked, and she hit play, heard a patient's voice, and spun to pick up her notepad to take notes.

❖

Rand pulled up in front of Jamie's small, mid-century patio home. Her home was just a few blocks away from her own, a luxury they took advantage of regularly. She let herself into the courtyard and the front door and stopped when she was greeted by Jamie's rescued beagles, Jackson and June. Jackson dropped and rolled over on his back for her to rub his stomach, and June careened into her with so much force she nearly fell over. Eventually, she made her way into the kitchen, where Jamie was cutting vegetables, a full salad bowl of leafy greens waiting and eggplant already breaded.

"This looks amazing."

"Right?" Jamie said with a nod. She wore a T-shirt with a superhero logo and jeans. Her head was freshly buzzed. Every inch of her arms were covered in tattoos, those she'd drawn herself, and those she'd collected from other artists. In her front room, where a couch should be, a massive canvas sat on a fabric tarp, braced by cinder blocks. Sitting at the counter, Rand was taken by it and told her so.

"You think?" Jamie asked, coming around to stand by her. "I've not moved it because it just doesn't feel quite right."

"Why?" Rand pointed at the flashes of color emerging from the center like they sprung from a black hole. "It's hopeful somehow." Rand tipped her head, moving her finger above the center of the piece to the edges. "All this color and light from darkness." Then she began to cry. It started abruptly, surprising even her, and she walked back to the counter to lean against it. Jamie wrapped her arms around her and rocked her.

"It's okay," she said again and again. Rand lost time. Her tears took her from regular space and deposited her somewhere else. At some point, the front door opened, and Rachel came, because when Rand returned, she was there too, sitting in front of her in a seat at the counter, holding her hands. Rachel smiled when they made eye contact and rose to wrap her arms around her and Jamie both. She wore her white-blond hair in a bun, tied tightly at the top of her head. Her contacts were in, but she wore no makeup, which meant she'd showered after she finished her shift at the hospital.

Then, Rachel cupped her face in her hands and kissed her forehead before pulling her fully into her arms. Jamie let go and walked around the counter. Rachel held Rand's head against her chest, standing to the side of her.

"You okay?" Rachel asked as Rand pulled away.

"I need to blow my nose," she said as she rounded the corner to the bathroom. Once she wiped ice-cold water on her face, blew her nose, and rinsed her mouth with Listerine, she paused to look in the mirror. Red eyes and nose stared back at her, and the small wrinkles around her lips and eyes looked new. Her curly hair grew haphazardly from her head, and she ran her hands through it, hoping it would settle. Once, she was cute, but now she was just tired. Back in the kitchen, she stopped at the edge of the counter. "I'm not sure where that came from."

Rachel said, "I think I have an idea." Rand studied the tile, hands on the side of the counter. "What happened, Rand?"

"Kim's parents sent me another letter."

"Oh, fuck me," Jamie said, slamming down the pan of eggplant. The dogs jumped. "Sorry. It's okay," she said as they ran to her, assuring them before she turned her attention back to Rand.

"My mom thinks I need to get more aggressive." Rachel looked at her with quiet compassion. Rand continued. "I wish they'd stop."

Jamie and Rachel stared at each other. Jamie shrugged, a movement Rand saw from the corner of her eyes. She knew it meant Jamie was deferring to Rachel. "Rand, can we help you? Can we do something?" It was Rachel who spoke, breaking the silence.

Rand sat down next to Rachel, who rubbed her back while she fought to regain control of her feelings. "I just want it to stop. So I can move on."

Jamie dropped the eggplant into the pan, the oil hissed, and Rand listened, focusing all her thoughts on it. Somehow, they'd arrived at forty. Rachel was a doctor, as planned, Rand a therapist, and Jamie did nothing, as planned. Tattoo artist, painter, sculptor, stained glass maker, chef, she'd made her own way in the world. "Can I have some coffee?" Rand wanted the warmth of it more than anything else.

Rachel arched her lower back as she walked around the counter, hand on it. Rand watched and assumed her back was sore. Rachel's job as an emergency room doctor and surgeon was physically taxing.

"Does your back hurt?"

"So much," Rachel said.

"You need some physical therapy," Rand said. Rachel ignored her.

Jamie reached for the pot, but Rachel caught her hand to let her know she would. Rand watched them together, their easy intimacy and friendship, and loved them both so dearly another bout of tears threatened.

"I love you both," Rand said.

"I know and it's mutual," Jamie said.

Rachel paused filling the coffee carafe with water and said, "I love you too. Both of you." She leaned into Jamie, shoulder to shoulder, and they fell into silence. No one knew what the answer was if Rand wouldn't let them help.

CHAPTER SIX

Shelley waited by the elevator; its constant beeping grated her nerves. She wondered how the receptionist could stand it, sitting there in front of it all day. Something fell, the crash echoing through the halls, followed by loud voices, and Shelley jumped. In an email a few months before, Rand suggested Shelley read a book called *The Highly Sensitive Person* by Elaine Aron. Shelley did, devouring it as if it unlocked at least fifty percent of her inner mysteries. She'd taken the advice in the book, and every subsequent documentary, article, and blog post about high sensitivity helped her find a new equilibrium, not entirely balanced, but more so than ever before.

She'd embraced her need for solitude and skipped family dinners because she didn't feel like attending. When she did see her family, Shelley imagined a great wall rising up around her. She'd learned that in a guided imagery book her search unearthed. The guided imagery book sent her into a wormhole, as she devoured books about Buddhism, Taoism, and then stumbled into modern mystics and psychoanalytical self-help. The previous six months had opened up more possibilities for

Shelley than her previous thirty-one years, and she greeted each day eager for more. A book by Thomas Merton about Zen and Christianity jostled in her bag.

The fallout from her appearance in April had been intense with her family, except for her youngest brother, Noah. He'd sent her a text with a thumbs-up and *Way to go. Rock the boat.* It was surprising, but she saved a screen shot of it and looked at it from time to time, as if organizing her strength around it and all the other new information she'd collected. She and her father had avoided one-on-one encounters since the show, so they'd not talked directly about it. She'd picked up her phone to call him multiple times and always stopped right before pressing his phone number. Instead, her siblings and mother represented their disappointment to her via phone calls and text messages. Eventually, the topic retreated, and some sense of quiet equilibrium resumed.

She'd been back to the television show half a dozen times to discuss a variety of issues, but none as charged as the topic with Rand. On a whim one night, while dining alone, she'd signed into Facebook and found Tony. He responded almost instantly, was in Manhattan, and she'd spent at least four weekends with him since. She was unraveling the truth of herself, pulling back the layers, one by one. To see who she really was, and what she really thought. On some level, avoidance of her father during this time of expansion and change made sense, and her therapist agreed.

"Shelley?" Someone called her name, and she turned to see Olivia, a camera tech, rushing toward her. "Hey. You busy? Wanna grab a drink with us?" Olivia had pink hair, tattoos on her arms, up to her neck, and massive gauges in her ears.

Shelley liked her, had noticed her during her first trip. She was hard to miss. They'd not spoken much, but Olivia was polite. Shelley hesitated, looked at her phone and the text from Tony saying his plane was delayed coming back from Chicago, and fought back a momentary sensation of panic about hanging out with the crew of the show.

"Uh, I guess. Where are you going?" Shelley stumbled over her words. Socializing was positive and healthy.

"Just a place around the corner. Hold on and we'll be right out."

Shelley stepped to the side of the elevator, back on the wall in the open spot between two plants. She heard, "Where'd she go? I swear I left her here."

"Here," Shelley said, from between the plants. "I'm here."

"You were plant incognito," another camera tech said.

"That wasn't the plan, but I suppose..." Shelley smiled and adjusted her bag. Others followed and they stepped into the elevator together, about seven in all, laughing at random observations of cast and crew. Shelley watched them in fascination as she always was at groups of friends, in easy camaraderie. She spoke little, falling to the side and the back of the group as they moved through the building, into the small bar around the corner, just as Olivia promised. Olivia waved her to sit next to her, and Shelley did.

The conversation swelled and Shelley struggled to follow it. Instead, she settled into a glass of wine, and then another, watching the group. Laughter, freedom, banter, and an undercurrent of something she couldn't quite identify. Olivia tugged at her arm, and Shelley jerked aware. "Yes?" She leaned closer to Olivia to hear.

"Come on. Let's get out of here. Take a walk?" Shelley looked around, shrugged, and collected her things. She'd not spoken once and was fine to leave. She followed Olivia from the crowded bar, wound outside, and was struck by the noise of the city, horns, sirens, wind, and voices. Olivia tugged her arm. "There is a better place we can sit and talk."

Shelley looked at her phone, wondering about Tony. They ducked into a bar. There was a rainbow flag above the mirror behind the counter. Olivia saw her look and said, "This okay?"

"Sure," Shelley said. "I have some time. I have plans with a friend, but he's delayed."

"Romantic?"

"Oh, no," Shelley clarified. "He's gay. We knew each other when we were young. Actually, dated for a while." Shelley blamed the wine for making her feel more open than normal. A ceiling fan buzzed and made a rocking sound as it moved. The door into the back of the bar grated as it opened and closed, a loud squeak, in need of lubricant.

A tall woman with long dark hair appeared in front of them. "Want a drink?"

"Yes. Red wine. Any kind. Not dry though," Shelley said.

Olivia ordered a martini, then turned to look at Shelley. "So?"

"What?"

"You're a lesbian, right?"

"I beg your pardon," Shelley said, shocked by the directness of the question.

"Who says 'beg your pardon'?" Olivia laughed at her and took a drink of the martini. "Come on. Are you? I'm dying to know."

Shelley picked up her wine and took a long drink. A hot flush raced over her body, and her instinct was to squirm away from the question. But in recent months, talking with Tony, attending therapy every week, she'd become more comfortable with her own feelings and discomfort. Taunya, her therapist, told her it was necessary to attend to the points of discomfort.

As an assignment, Shelley was to acknowledge the discomfort and desire to retreat first, and then detach from it, watch it objectively, and observe and name its components. For someone like Shelley, a highly sensitive, rational introvert, with obsessive-compulsive tendencies, it was the perfect task, simultaneously providing an escape hatch from overpowering emotions while promoting self-awareness.

In this moment, Shelley wanted to flee. Instead, she took a deep breath and spoke with honesty. "I'm not really ready to discuss that openly."

Olivia looked at her, her pierced right eyebrow raised, and then took another sip of her drink. "I've noticed you since you first came on the show. Wanted to spend time together. I'm glad we're doing this."

Shelley felt uncertain, but smiled at the compliment, and upon seeing the news on television, turned the conversation to politics. She peppered Olivia with questions, not surprised to learn she was a Democratic socialist. Their conversation wound to music, books, and Shelley momentarily forgot herself and ordered yet another glass of wine. She paused to check her phone and saw Tony's plane had landed. "I need to get going," Shelley said, lifting her bag from the back of her chair. Olivia reached up, grabbed the sides of her hoodie, and leaned forward.

"Want a kiss to see if you like it?" Shelley looked into her eyes, stunned, uncertain, and froze. Olivia kissed her lightly before she could answer. Shelley lifted her hand to her lips. Olivia was in front of her, but she saw Rand's eyes at dinner, their soft questioning, remembered her hands as she opened the door for her at the restaurant, arm around the back of the bench in Times Square, and their embrace at the end of the night.

"I—I'm sorry. I need to go." Shelley was flushed from the wine. "I—" She stammered and wished for her legal calm. "Thanks for tonight." She left with a glance over her shoulder at Olivia, stepping into the emerging darkness. She texted Tony and told him she was on her way. Serendipitously, she caught the subway just as the door closed. Shelley pressed against the space between the bench and the door, her back against the train wall.

She squirmed thinking about Olivia kissing her. Her lips were soft, though the contact brief. Shelley didn't find her particularly attractive, but had only ever kissed men, and slept with just one, in desperation during her mid-twenties. She wanted nothing more than for the young man to cure her of the blank nothingness she felt inside. Instead, it made her feel worse, more damaged and broken. All romantic experiences left her hollow, unmoved, and certain she held some deep unresolvable defect. She'd noticed Olivia but didn't want to become involved that way. She liked attending the show, and her presence would complicate matters for her.

Shelley also knew little about her and wasn't certain of her intentions. Shelly wondered if she should be more offended by the kiss, as there was no consent first. Then, she thought honestly about the night and how she opened to her when they talked, listened more closely than she did normally. Shelley felt enough attraction to follow her to a bar. She put her hand on her stomach, confused and sickened. Human relationships felt taxing, exhausting, and dangerous at times, from those with her family to everyone else. Except Rand.

Rand felt safe, and warmth spread through her at just the thought of her.

The street names flickered across the neon boards above the doors. Despite her drama, the earth made another rotation in its journey, suspended in space and time. Shelley pondered gravity and the ground under her feet, on a planet, circling the sun, in a corner of a galaxy in an unfathomable universe.

It was possible a creator God made it, or it was possible it emerged in space and time spontaneously, ineffably, and she'd never understand it. Her anxiety about the kiss evaporated, and she breathed, finding comfort in her finitude, insignificance. The tight tension in her chest released, like a rubber band held back and let go. Her stop arrived and she took the stairs from the subway carefully, a little tipsy from the wine. On the street, her pace quickened.

A chill descended, and she zipped her hoodie as a rush of wind pushed against her. Tony's apartment was only a few blocks more. She was captivated by the noises of the city and listened to the sounds of taxi horns and conversations.

She forgot to count the steps to Tony's apartment. Her phone rang as she put the key in the apartment door. Struggling with bag, key, and phone, she answered the call one-handed, not looking to see who it was. "Shelley, what did you do?" It was Noah.

She dropped her bag and smiled at Tony. "Hold on." Tony hugged her. "Noah," she said to Tony.

"Tell him I said hi," Tony said.

"I heard him," Noah said from the other side of the phone. "Shelley, what did you do?"

"What are you talking about? Do what?"

"You don't know?" Noah's voice was full of confusion and hurt, but Shelley ignored it.

"I really don't, and I need to go. I just got here with Tony and want to see him. We can talk when I get home."

"No. Wait. Just check your text messages."

"Okay," Shelley said. She hung up the phone, silenced it, and tossed it into her purse. She'd check her text messages later. "How was your trip?"

"Are you drunk?"

"A little. But I'm fine. It was a weird night," Shelley said.

"You're breaking all the rules." Tony's hair recently bleached, square jaw overgrown with stubble, blue eyes alive with joy as he poured more wine.

Shelley laughed and they fell into easy conversation where she shared her encounter with Olivia.

CHAPTER SEVEN

When Shelley returned home in October, the internet gutted her life and left her stranded on the outside, looking in while its momentum ran its course. The photo of Olivia kissing her went viral within hours. Olivia had a friend follow them to the bar and snap the photo. It had all been staged to humiliate her and force her out of the closet. Shelley deactivated her social media accounts, changed her phone number, and refused to discuss anything with anyone—except her therapist.

She quit her job at the small corporate law firm where she'd worked amidst her other political activities for the previous few years. Her coworkers said nothing, but she felt skinless. It was time to move on and she knew it. She left quietly and no one tried to stop her.

She saw her therapist twice a week. For weeks, she spoke in circles about how she felt. Violated, attacked, provoked, betrayed, humiliated, a victim of social cancel culture, where contrary ideas were beat into submission without reciprocal conversation. Taunya told her she was a victim of the intense partisan environment of America, where each side viewed the other as enemies.

Together they unraveled her crippling fear, the reasons endless—her father, patriarchal Christianity, the projection of it onto her relationship with God, life, and the Universe, and the way she used it all to restrict her deepest truths. Finally, one afternoon just before Thanksgiving, Shelley found the space to celebrate her freedom. Taunya pointed out that Shelley had begun this path on her own the previous year. Olivia, her deception, the photo was morally bankrupt, unfair, but could be leveraged to begin the life she wanted.

When Taunya said this, her moment of clarity emerged. She'd been to at least five therapists before meeting her. Something about Taunya put her at ease and on notice. Shelley sensed Taunya was her intellectual equal, and as well as being openly gay, she exuded feminine warmth. Taunya gave her hope during each session. She saw herself in Taunya, who crossed her legs at the ankles, wore dark suits, and preferred centrist politics. She'd married her partner of twenty years as soon as she was able.

She listened to Shelley with compassion and interest, softly encouraging her journey toward herself, without judgment and contempt.

What was it about the other that allows us to see ourselves? Without them, we are lost, Shelley thought. We greet the other and, in the friend, we find pieces of our own soul. How could such sacred reality exist in the same time and space continuum where human relationships were so taxing and dangerous? How could she exist with such cognitive dissonance?

"So, I'm gay," Shelley said out loud, for the first time. Taunya met her proclamation with a wide smile and walked to kneel in front of her. She hugged her, perhaps an unorthodox move for a therapist, but one Shelley appreciated. She cried, sitting on the couch in Taunya's office, her arms wrapped around her.

"Yes," Taunya said. "You are. What you do with that now is up to you. Who you tell. How you manage it."

As Shelley's tears abated, Taunya moved back to her chair.

"I'd like to talk to my dad." Taunya grimaced, and Shelley saw it. "You think it's a bad idea?"

"He matters a great deal to you, and you have the benefit of already knowing how he feels about it. What he thinks. What his beliefs are. Are you prepared for rejection?"

Shelley was in silent agreement, the truth painful in her gut. "I've denied who I am for thirty-one years because I knew it would devastate him."

"I'm afraid you're not so powerful you can devastate another person by living authentically. He's responsible for himself, including the constructs he creates to live his life by."

Constructs. The word raced through her. "Religion is a construct," Shelley said.

"I think so," Taunya said. "It's a myth. We're amazing storytellers. It helps us build civilizations. Get along in big groups. We build constructs, from governments to religions, so we can cooperate. It's what makes us the dominant species on earth."

"Of course we do," Shelley said, gaze unfixed, her consciousness reorganizing around the new information. "I think I need to talk to him."

The clock said their time was up. Taunya stood to follow her to the door. "Call me if you need anything after. Anytime, anything." Shelley agreed, lost in thought. It was late and her steps echoed in the empty office building. She opened the door at the bottom of the stairs, and a reporter took her picture, a strong flash in her eyes.

"Shelley Whitmore. Want to come out? Talk about your sexuality?"

Shelley ignored the shadowy figure behind the blinding flashes and rushed to her car, unlocking the door via remote in route. She jumped in, reversed the car, and hoped whomever it was moved. She'd had a dozen or more encounters since the incident with Olivia. She shouldn't have been so preoccupied with therapy she didn't look outside before plunging into darkness.

Shelley dialed her father's number. He answered on the first ring.

"Shelley," he said quickly.

"Dad." She paused, voice and heart heavy. "Can I see you? Can we talk?"

"Of course. I'm home."

"Be there soon," she said and hung up.

Her father loomed large in her psyche, a towering figure who defined the parameters of her life's experience. Her emotions for him were a tangled web of love and fear, and she longed for his favor and acceptance. She was the smartest of her siblings and the only one who kept pace with his rapid-fire questioning over meals. "What year was the Constitution drafted? When do Biblical scholars agree the earth was created? What year did Constantine decree Catholicism was to be the empire's religion? How do we justify the creation of Protestantism as something other than a cultural and relativist act?"

Shelley could answer them all, one after another, and as she grew older, often dared to disagree with him, but only so far. An invisible boundary existed where she knew her intellect was not allowed. In recent months, Shelley wondered if he knew or sensed who she was and could not bring himself to face it.

When her mother accused him of favoring Shelley, he'd deny it, but then wink. As a child, he'd been her best friend. He spoiled her, took her to conferences, meetings, and events. He began explaining complicated legal issues to her when she was just eight years old. He encouraged her questions and growing intellectual confidence, proud of her capacity to win any verbal argument he staged for her, with himself or friends.

When she won first place in her middle school debates, he was there, clapping with love and pride in his eyes. Her mother paled next to him in Shelley's memory, mind, and heart. When Shelley saw inside a slaughterhouse on a school field trip at the age of sixteen and announced she would no longer eat meat, her father supported her and spoke at length about animal welfare at church the next Sunday, making an argument for veganism in the Garden of Eden.

Her three older brothers and two older sisters married, bought homes in the same neighborhood, and had families of their own. Noah was still at Liberty University, unmarried, but unlike her, in his early twenties. Shelley couldn't articulate or explain her need for solitude, or her lack of desire for marriage, so she stopped trying.

A silent acquiescence descended on the topic somewhere around her thirtieth birthday, but it signaled the growing chasm between her and her father. The space made her heart ache, though she pressed forward, a silent and invisible urge propelling her. The destination was unknown, but with all of her being, she hoped her father would join her on the other side of her discovery. She loved him and he gave her so much of what she valued in herself.

The drive to her childhood home felt endless. Every stop light agitated her and she was overwhelmed by each traffic stop and slow-moving car. She drove eighty-five on a stretch of open highway. When she finally turned onto the street, just twenty-five minutes had passed, but it felt like two weeks. Taunya would not agree with this, but it needed to be over so she could move on.

Shelley parked in the driveway. Her dad had turned on the bright floodlights for her and left the garage door open. The deep trees around them moved in a slight breeze, casting shadows across the driveway. She walked past his dark BMW and slipped off her shoes at the door. She closed the garage door behind and called out from the laundry room.

"It's me," Shelley said. Her mom was at the kitchen counter, laptop open, scrolling Facebook. Shelley hugged her and felt deep sadness. Tears queued up behind her eyes, ready to come out.

"Are you hungry?" Her mother rubbed the top of Shelley's arms and tucked a strand of hair behind her ear. "Can I make you something?" Shelley hugged her again, holding the dark braid at the base of her Mom's neck.

"No, I'm okay, but thanks. I love you, Mom," Shelley said.

"I love you too, honey." Her mom turned back to Facebook Shelley put her hand on the kitchen counter. "You paint?" Her mom closed the laptop. "A week ago. Do you like it?"

"I do," Shelley said.

Her mom stared at her. She'd seen the photo, Shelley was sure, but didn't know if she should address it. She'd refused all phone calls, hadn't responded to a single text message, and was sure she'd ignored a visit at her front door the week prior. One of the benefits of being an adult was being able to decide when to talk to people.

"Well, did you want to talk or…" she trailed off.

"Is Dad here too?"

"I'll go get him. Get something to drink." Shelley watched her mom walk from the kitchen. She walked to the fridge, pulled out a soda, held it, put it back in, and then walked to the Keurig and made a cup of coffee. Her parents were in the kitchen as she took her first sip.

Shelley joined them at the kitchen table. Her father kissed her head as he sat. She made eye contact with a small smile. He acknowledged it and settled into the chair. Shelley spent so much time worrying how she would feel, it'd not occurred to her that he'd be scared. She saw it on his face, in the strained expression in his eyes, the tightness in his mouth, and the way he clenched his teeth. She did the same thing, she thought.

"I've not answered calls or texts. I'm sorry for that. I've needed some time." Shelley hadn't planned on what to say, and now words failed her. "I'm not really sure what to say."

"What happened?" Her father spoke finally, hands in front of him on the table.

"I went out with the crew after the show. Then Olivia set up the photo."

"It was set up?" His relief was evident.

"It was." Shelley wanted to stop there because the energy of the room lifted. Her mother sighed. Her father held her wrist in his big hand.

"I knew it, Whitney. Didn't I say it?" he said to her mom, who smiled.

"Dad," Shelley said, lifting the mug to take a drink. "Wait, though. I'm not done."

He pulled his hand from her wrist, the tension back in his face. "The picture was staged, but the rumors are true."

"No," he said, standing. He took a glass from the cupboard, filled it with water, and drank it in two gulps.

"Dad," Shelley said. "Please come back."

"Shelley," her mom said. "You're just confused. Why don't you come stay with us? Let your apartment go. Let us take care of you for a little while."

Her dad agreed, and Shelley set down the coffee mug and held her face in her hands, gathering her courage.

"That's not an option," Shelley said. She thought about Rand in Times Square, sitting next to her on the bench. The light lit up her gray-green eyes, and when she smiled at Shelley, small lines around her eyes crinkled to life.

"Shelley," her dad said, now back at the table. "Please reconsider this path. I think you've struggled so much because it's out of alignment with God's plan for us all. You know better. You've always known better. It's a burden for you to carry, like we all have burdens. God gives us nothing more than we can carry."

Shelley breathed out and closed her eyes, marshaling her resources. "It's not a burden," she said, eyes heavy with fatigue and sadness. Taunya was right. She wasn't ready for this.

She looked at her mom first, then her dad. She met and held his eyes. She remembered him taking her to work with him, the legal briefs he let her read. Remembered stopping at the ice cream store on a Saturday afternoon, holding his hand as they waited in line. Saw him beaming at her law school graduation, clapping feverishly when she won her first litigation case.

"I love you so much," Shelley said to him. He reached out to touch her arm, affirming.

"I love you, too," he said. "So does Mom." Her mom agreed and touched her other arm.

"If I am who you want me to be," Shelley said, "I can't be who I am. It's killing me. I would rather die." She spoke so truthfully with so much earnest emotion they both sat back. Shelley took her cup to the sink, rinsed it, and returned to them. She kissed her father on the cheek, and then her mother. She paused before leaving the house and met her father's eyes.

"I'm not doing this to hurt you. I want you to be in my life." Her father stared, eyes moist with tears. "But I can't not be who I am anymore. It's just not possible." She paused in the garage as she waited for the door to rise. She walked to her car, head down, and behind the steering wheel, looked up to see her father at the end of his car, half in the garage, a part of him obscured by the floodlight. She turned away from him and put the car in drive.

❖

Shelley ate a pint of coconut cookie dough ice cream. She'd lost a few pounds in the week since the photo appeared, her appetite fickle like her emotions, and she felt justified binging her favorite comfort food. She was thoroughly alone on the other side of the conversation with her parents and longed for any sort of company to reassure her the world beyond was still alive and worth exploring.

She picked up her phone, checked email, and was relieved to see a message from Rand. Rand replied within hours to every email message she sent, whether it was about the book she'd read about intuitive healing, a new Netflix original, or an abstract philosophical thought she wanted to share. An email chain about the problem of evil consumed them for three weeks. They bantered back and forth about the possibility of God given the problem of evil and suffering in the world. Rand insisted it disqualified a creator, but Shelley wasn't ready to let go of hope.

Shelley hadn't wanted to share her crippling anxiety or depression, not that Rand would have minded. She really wanted to send a long email about the anguish of disappointing her father. But she didn't. Her goal was to come to terms with all of it, straighten and bring order to her own internal life before she acted on any of the impulses she felt when she thought about Rand.

She'd also not discussed the photo, though Rand must have heard about it. The picture flooded social media. Meme generators worked overtime with it. Shelley googled her own name one day and spent an hour clicking through images, reading all the parodies the world created at her expense. She breathed through the humiliation, reminded of St. Teresa de Avila, who encouraged her disciples to embrace moments of humiliation to grow closer to God. Most of the memes took aim at her father and his organization as they rightly should. It was difficult to feel wronged or outraged, even as hot shame and a blanket of helplessness settled on her. Was it even possible Rand could want her, given all of what was true about her life and beliefs?

Shelley always responded to Rand via her laptop, making certain to address every detail of the original email. She wanted Rand to know she'd read every word and every detail was important to her. While other people flirted or expressed sexual interest, Shelley organized words into balanced sentences, perfectly aligned with the flow of Rand's thoughts. As she sat looking at the email, Shelley wanted to say, "Since the moment I saw you, I think about you all the time." But those words would never come from her, at least not yet.

Hitting send was an act of courage, each time she did it, whether the email was about a book she read upon Rand's suggestion or the details of a childhood memory.

After the email disappeared into the ether, Shelley felt resolved sadness. She'd lose her family, her father's approval, but she'd give life a shot on her own terms. The emptiness of her apartment closed in, so she turned off the lights and took her laptop with her to bed. She'd take the anxiety medication Taunya gave her for moments like this and let the day end. Tomorrow, she'd figure out what came next.

❖

When Shelley opened her eyes the next morning, she shuffled to the kitchen, poured a cup of coffee with soy creamer, and promptly went back to bed. She propped pillows behind her and opened her laptop. Rand hadn't replied yet, but it was just after four a.m. her time. Shelley reread the story in Rand's most recent email about her mom and smiled as she moved it to a folder titled, "R Emails."

She browsed the *Economist*, *New York Times*, *Washington Post*, and *Forbes*, consciously avoiding Twitter. She tried to read a book about evangelicalism Taunya recommended she read, but couldn't focus. She snuggled under the blankets, coffee cup between her hands, groggy from the medication, but too alert to go back to sleep.

Shelley was only about fourteen when she realized God was not engaging with her on the particulars of every moment like her classmates claimed. Jesus was not ever present in her life. Instead, he was either a mythical boogeyman or evidence of her first great failure in connection. She always felt a reserved distance between herself and the evangelicalism that fueled her family's passionate engagement with the world. Taunya suggested it was her intelligence and personality typology.

Shelley wrote this to Rand, her only mention of therapy, and Rand wrote back, in complete agreement. Rand was raised agnostic, attended multiple churches, and read the sacred texts of all world religions with her mom as bedtime stories. Her heart ached when she thought about Rand's parents, and their existence made her silently long for something more for herself.

She imagined sitting down to read the Upanishads with her father. Imagined sharing coffee while they discussed the

Quran. He'd likely be entertained by the activity but would evaluate the material through the lens of his previously accepted construct of reality. Shelley embraced the word construct again, made it her own, and then pulled it apart in her mind's eye.

She had to make changes. Needed to get free of her family. Shelley decided what her next step would be. Around noon, she called Nate Finnigan, the Executive Director of Landed Liberty, a Libertarian think tank in Phoenix.

He'd offered her a job the year before, and she declined gracefully. Now, she hoped he'd consider her again. He answered her call immediately and sent the employment offer via email within the day. She accepted and her energy lifted.

She wanted space, time, and open sky to figure out what was next. Maybe that's why a Libertarian think tank in the American west was so appealing. If her aim was to find herself, understand who she was as an individual, she couldn't think of a better place to do it. She'd heard someone say that people moved to Los Angeles and Phoenix to disappear into a sea of other individuals. Phoenix, in particular, felt promising to her. It was the fifth largest city in the United States, where houses had six-foot-high brick fences, so no one was forced to talk to their neighbors. It was Barry Goldwater's neighborhood where the first rule of law was to mind your own business and pay your taxes.

It sounded heavenly to Shelley.

It was also where Rand lived.

❖

Shelley sat on Tony's couch, feet tucked under her, laptop open. A winter chill filled the small apartment, despite the radiator running on high. She'd finished at MSNBC and was surprised to find that Olivia was no longer employed there. Greg shared that he asked her to move on, voluntarily, about a week after the photo was posted on social media and it became clear what her intentions were. Shelley thanked him but was upset Olivia lost her job. Taunya would say there were natural consequences to decisions we make, and Shelley held this thought, working it through with her feelings. Perhaps Olivia was a natural consequence of the choices she'd made.

Either way, or any way, or in every way, Olivia had freed her, and for that reason Shelley felt a debt of gratitude, even if those around her didn't feel the same way. Shelley scrolled through her email, stopping at Rand's reply. Rand had watched her on MSNBC earlier and Shelley's face burned. She imagined Rand watching her on television, sitting on a couch, in a front room she only imagined, and Shelley hoped she looked and sounded okay.

Rand told her she disagreed with her perspective on taxes and social responsibility. Shelley opened her email and began to write back. It was time to tell her she'd accepted a job in Phoenix, but she was nervous about it, worried Rand would view it as an intrusion.

Shelley replied in her organized and consistent way to Rand's email and added the details of her job offer and relocation. Rand had pressed a more commutation perspective on taxes than Shelley would embrace, and told her so, so Shelley wrote, "When you entrust institutions with global reach, like government, with application of moral principles, you have to trust they will always operate with integrity, be capable of change, and available for feedback. Have you spent time at the DMV?" She smiled as she wrote the last question, teasing, prodding.

"I think many liberals fled to the Democratic Party because of social issues, but there really is a bridge to common ground around individual liberty. I just want individuals to have freedom to move without intrusion. Social liberalism doesn't just belong to Democrats any more so than God belongs to conservatives. Isn't it possible to find a third way?" Shelley wanted the third way, for herself and her country. She read and reread her email, and then pressed send before there was too much time to think about it.

"Hello, my news star." Tony opened the door and came to her.

She made room for him to sit next to her. "Did you watch?"

"I hate the news," he said, belligerent. "But yes. You're clearly wrong about everything, though I don't want to ruin a perfectly good friendship because you're a silly Republican."

"That's a dirty word these days."

"You did it to yourselves. You're so mean. Jump off the ship, dear," Tony said. Then he pulled his phone out and scrolled through Facebook. "What are we doing? Want to see a jazz concert tonight? I can get us free tickets."

"I thought you had a date," Shelley said.

"Ghosted. He heard I'm friends with a Republican."

"Stop it." Shelley swatted at him.

"Okay, he didn't. But he did cancel, and I feel fickle now." Tony faced her. "Were you writing to Rand?" he teased her, smirk on his face.

"I do other things with my laptop," Shelley said. Tony raised a bleached eyebrow. He dyed it for his current off-Broadway role. "Yes, okay? She watched me on MSNBC."

"I'm sure she did," he said with a smile. "We need to work on your hair and general attire. You need some color in your wardrobe."

"We've had this conversation since we were adolescents," Shelley said.

"And you're still not listening." Shelley sighed and looked down at her jeans and plain black sweater. She wouldn't openly concede he was right, but had thought more about it lately.

"Let's go shopping." He clapped. "Get some food, try on clothes. I'm poor but you can buy me something." They left together, arm in arm, the city alive around them, even as the air blew cold.

Tony made Shelley stop for a new hairstyle. Her hair fell in layers around her face, and she glimpsed her reflection in the window. She paused and looked directly at herself.

"What are you thinking, dear?" Tony was behind her, hands on her shoulders.

"I didn't grimace when I saw myself." He smiled and kissed her cheek and wrapped his arms around her shoulders. "Thank you for not giving up on me." A wave of gratitude and deep emotion spilled through her chest like a hot cup of coffee knocked across an empty countertop. Tony saw it and let go and held an arm around her waist as they walked.

"Well, I hate to tell you I might if we don't do something about your clothes now. I'm trying to make it as an actor, and there are standards if I am to be seen in public with you."

Shelley laughed at his teasing and let him lead her into a boutique where she purchased a bright red suit, at his insistence, and a few new blouses. They settled into the back of a darkened movie theater together after they were finished, giggling like teenagers at the complicated foreign art film.

Tony said, "This film is making me a Republican." Shelley laughed and raised her hands in confusion. "I mean, it's so complicated I just want apple pie, baseball, and a stroll down a nineteen fifties small town Main Street wearing a poodle skirt."

CHAPTER EIGHT

The bright sun filtered through the open blinds on the sliding door and spread through Shelley's small living room. She didn't own much and had finally unpacked. She found an apartment she liked near work online, rented it sight unseen, sold her furniture, shipped her books, clothes, and bedding, and then got in her car and drove across the country in January.

Shelley took her time, and for the first time in her life, forgot to count anything. She picked up I-40 West just inside Tennessee and meandered slowly to Phoenix, stopping where compelled, taking notes, journaling. As she watched the landscape unfold, an idea for a book began to form—a journey to self across the country. She found an extended stay just outside Memphis and settled in for three weeks and felt anonymous and invisible. She wrote, slept, and walked through the city streets.

She finished the outline for the book there. She delivered multiple articles to Nate for publication, reacting to Supreme Court rulings and popular news without leaving her hotel room. She left Memphis and stopped in Little Rock for another three weeks. By the time she left there, half of the story was written.

She was still unsure where the story should go next. Her next destination was Santa Rosa, New Mexico, where the endless expanse of western sky greeted her each morning. She stayed two months there, and countless hours in front of the hotel room window, in awe of the rolling hills and clear, endless blue sky.

Something in her shifted in the long, detached solitude. Away from her family and familiar environment, Shelley found a new voice. It began to show itself in her writing. Nate commented on it. As did Rand, in the emails they exchanged day after day. Shelley wanted to see Rand again, but needed more time to organize her new self into something she understood. Shelley didn't want to project any of her struggle on Rand.

She'd finally arrived in Phoenix in late April. The apartment manager allowed the shipping company inside her apartment to drop off the boxes. She'd spent her first few days in Arizona shopping for a couch, television, kitchen supplies, and bed. Shelley settled into work, avoided her father's recent phone calls. She finally texted him to let him know she was safe but asked for space. He responded that he'd read her articles and was impressed and would welcome a conversation about any of them at any time.

Shelley wondered about the human capacity to compartmentalize. While she'd done it for years, it had nearly killed her, but in the absence of acceptance from her dad, it seemed like she might have to accept that was what he was capable of and make peace with it. But she wasn't ready for that yet. How she felt sitting at their kitchen table in the late fall was still too vivid.

Shelley texted Rand. She'd been in town almost two weeks. There were really no more excuses why she'd not reached out except that she was nervous. She'd not seen her since the night they shared the previous spring in New York City. It took just a moment for Rand to respond, inviting her for coffee the next morning. Since she'd met Rand, besides emailing her every day, Shelley read her three books, dozens of scholarly articles, and watched every video of her on YouTube.

Rand was a recognized thought leader in transgender support, and a fierce advocate for transgender children. Shelley learned so much about herself, and Rand, while reading her words, and her body pulsed with excitement at the idea of seeing her again. As her heart raced and face flushed, Shelley openly acknowledged her crush on Rand. To some, it might seem insignificant. To Shelley, it was like hiking Kilimanjaro.

❖

Shelley changed clothes five times. Finally, she settled on a pair of dark jeans and a new lightweight red blouse. The stress of her photo had taken off about ten of her extra forty pounds, and she felt better about herself. She brushed her hair, and then tied it back. It was too hot to wear down and felt too formal. She began to put in her contacts, but then paused and chose her glasses. She remembered Rand when she opened the door to her dressing room the previous spring. Rand said she liked her glasses. Her eyes felt dry and tired anyway, though that wasn't entirely true.

Shelley rushed down the stairs, suddenly afraid of being late, but easily found the coffee shop Rand suggested. She'd stared at the map as she drank her morning cup of coffee, memorizing the route. Despite her worry, she was fifteen minutes early, but it was too hot to sit in the car. The blistering heat of summer was already on its way. In just a few short weeks since her arrival, the temperature had risen from a peaceful, perfect eighty to a heavy, angry one hundred degrees plus. Because she wasn't used to it, her lips chapped and her eyes burned, and she definitely needed to drink more water.

She found a table in the far corner of the shop and ordered coffee from the server, but asked to wait for anything else. The menu looked delicious, with vegan muffins, pancakes, and tofu breakfast burritos. Rand had picked well and thoughtfully, and then she saw her crossing the parking lot. Rand wore a pair of shorts, canvas shoes, and a T-shirt. Shelley looked at her strong hands swinging by her side, and a flush stole up her neck, which she silently willed down. Rand opened the door and saw her, an earnest smile on her face. Shelley waved and stood as Rand approached. Rand hugged her and she stiffened momentarily, afraid she'd swoon and give herself away, but then relaxed as Rand pulled away with a smile.

"You look tired," Shelley said before she thought. She looked older than Shelley remembered, with more gray in her short hair, and dark circles round her eyes. "Are you okay?" Shelley forgot all her nervousness.

"I, uh…" Rand stumbled. "It's been a rough few days." Shelley was unsure what to say. But she waited, silent, head tipped.

"My dead wife's parents keep sending me letters. They think I'm keeping family heirlooms from them. Now they just sued me. I got it on Friday." Rand wiped her hand over her face. "God, Shelley, I'm so sorry. I feel overly emotional and exposed already, and I didn't even ask if you were in the space to take that on." Outside, someone slammed a car door. Loud voices followed, with laughter, and a horn beeped from the intersection near them. Rand's gaze was drawn to the door and the commotion outside.

But Shelley wasn't listening to the noise, for once, or to her apology. Instead, she asked, "How long has this been going on now?"

"Three years. Letters. Calls. Constant harassment. Every month. Now a lawsuit."

"Why won't this get resolved?"

"They want an outcome that isn't possible." Rand called the server. "Let's order. You'll love the food." Shelley ordered a tofu burrito. "We don't have to talk about this right now."

"No, it's fine." Shelley was engaged and not to be deterred. "Unless you don't want to anymore. I think I can help, if you want."

CHAPTER NINE

Surprised, Rand quieted as the server poured their coffee. She cupped it in her hands. She didn't want to entangle Shelley or anyone else in her mess. But she was tired, emotional, and desperate for the long struggle to end. First, she'd watched Kim die, rapidly, her body wasting away in just months. She'd grieved, and remained trapped in heavy guilt, which wound around her legs like barbwire and prevented her from moving forward.

Rand put her hand on her chest, over her heart and above her solar plexus chakra. Shelley was a lawyer, and from their ongoing correspondence, Rand knew she was thoughtful, honest, and deliberate. And she was looking at her with such kind eyes.

"Help me," Rand said in a rush, the grief perched in her chest, unmoving, a winged monster who moved in and refused to leave. "Everyone tells me I should get more aggressive. Or it won't stop. But I don't want to fight. I just want it to end."

Shelley acted like she would touch her, but then pulled her hands back into her lap. "I'll fix it for you," she said.

"Why would you help me? You barely know me," Rand asked, picking at her food.

"Some Republicans have hearts," Shelley said with a laugh, and Rand smiled at her. Rand had teased her with that line a week before. "We're not all evil. Some of us just think the government should remain small."

"Do you still?" Rand asked, thinking about the photo Rachel and Jamie showed her over dinner a few months before as they teased her about their ongoing correspondence.

"Yes, I think so. There's danger in the centralization of power. But there's space for compromise to move forward," Shelley's answer was slow and deliberate, her gaze drifting off in thought as she considered her answer. Rand watched it with affection and some surprise because she felt no urge to argue with Shelley.

"The key is to balance the legitimate fear of power centralization with the urge to evolve in other ways. Honestly, the problem with any institution is people. If human motives were pure, altruistic, and concerned for the common good it wouldn't matter what government we had. If we could truly self-regulate, we'd be past these petty squabbles," Shelley said.

"I don't think I've ever thought of it that way," Rand said, compelled by a sudden urge to be closer without conscious consideration. She retreated and wondered if Shelley noticed. Shelley's attention was diverted by a noise at the counter.

"So, that means you think some regulation is necessary?" Rand felt better in Shelley's presence. She watched Shelley sip her coffee and grin shyly at her attention. Rand thought about reaching across the table to grab her hands but didn't.

"Yes. I'm not a Tea Party Republican. I'm pragmatic. I think my point is that any unchecked power is dangerous." Shelley smiled at the server who set her food down.

"Then that same sentiment is true for the unbridled power of the private corporations and billionaires," Rand said. "It can't just be about government."

Shelley's eyes were unfixed in thought. Rand liked the expression on her face when she considered a perspective. She also admired it. Shelley forced her to check her own preconceived notions about who people were. "That's valid, Rand. I'd like to think more about it."

"Of course," Rand said. "I'll expect follow-up." They smiled at each other, and it was Rand who broke eye contact first.

"Thank you for letting me help you." Shelley's voice was quiet, unassuming.

"Thank you for helping me." Rand met Shelley's eyes, their dark brown unsettling, and she struggled to maintain contact. So many other people offered her help, and she told them no. But for some reason, Shelley's help seemed prudent and unobtrusive and she wanted it. Why was as big a mystery as all their contact before.

"Can I have copies of the previous correspondence?"

"Yeah, I have them all at home in a box." They ate in some silence, moments broken up by comments about the food, heat, and Shelley's relocation. They didn't linger long, and as the server left the check, Rand reached into her pocket. Shelley moved toward it as well, but Rand stopped her. "Can I buy? It seems the least I can do for your help."

"My help has no fee or obligation attached," Shelley said in that maddeningly calm and quiet way she always spoke, as if each word she uttered bore the weight of all the cosmos's intentions.

"I like the way you talk," Rand said, surprising herself.

"Is it my accent?" Shelley asked, face lit up with the compliment.

"No. Maybe. You're just mindful and deliberate." Rand grinned at the blush in Shelley's cheeks. "So, I'll still buy, if that's okay." Shelley accepted her generosity and they rose to leave. Rand held open the door for her, and they walked outside together. The sun's rays were unrelenting. Shelley shielded her eyes to talk, and Rand reached for her, hand on her arm and turned them so Shelley faced away from the sun. Rand pulled her sunglasses off her shirt where she'd tucked them and put them on.

"Thank you," Shelley said.

"Are you busy now?" Rand asked, a little surprised by the eagerness she felt about Shelley coming home with her.

"No. This is all I have planned today," Shelley said.

"I live just up the road. I could give you the paperwork. We could continue the conversation."

"I can follow you?" Rand agreed and they left together, their cars moving toward Rand's house. As the mountain preserve came into view, Rand wondered if Shelley appreciated the patch of desert in the middle of the urban sprawl and wanted to ask her. She was proud to take her home. Rand's house was Santa Fe style with a small courtyard and rounded arches that were covered in mosaic tile. A fountain splashed just inside the gate. The neighborhood was planned, controlled, maintained, and Rand felt safe and settled.

Rand's garage was a mess, but Shelley didn't comment on it. "Your home is beautiful," Shelley said from the driveway, standing by her car.

"I really like it. A bit of peace in the noise."

"The development is charming. So much character." Shelley looked down the street, turning in full circle.

Rand had been watching her, noting the curve of her breasts under her blouse and the soft roundness of her stomach. Confused by the rush of attraction she felt, Rand turned and took a deep, steadying breath and waved her in. "Come inside," she said as she opened the door into the house from the garage. From the garage, they stepped through a small laundry room.

"The tile is gorgeous," Shelley said, looking down at dark brown terra-cotta tile that stretched through the entire home.

"What are you doing here?" While surprised, Rand's voice betrayed amusement, and Shelley looked up just in time to stop herself from colliding with Rand.

"We used your pool." Jamie laughed, dripping water on the tile in front of the fridge. "I sent you a text." Rand pointed at the puddle. "Oh, yeah. I'll clean that up." Jamie looked behind Rand, eyebrow raised. "Who is this?"

Rand stepped to the side. "Shelley Whitmore, meet Jamie Gonzales, my best friend without boundaries."

"That is really dramatic," Jamie said walking carefully toward Shelley across the wet tile. "I might bust my ass."

"You'd deserve it," Rand shot back to her. "Ah, the beagles are here!" She opened the sliding glass door.

"Rachel, isn't the water still cold?" Rand said from her bent position by the door with the beagles, who now turned to Shelley, but Rachel wouldn't get a chance to answer. Shelley bent and was wet with wild doggy kisses from one while the other jumped into her arms with such force she fell backward on the floor with them while they climbed on her. She laughed with pure joy, and Rand leaned forward to grab one of them, who wiggled in an attempt to get back to Shelley.

Jamie whistled and they both settled. She held out her hand to Shelley, who used it to stand back up. "They are usually better behaved than that. I think they like you." Shelley smiled as she watched them rush by Rand back out the door, chasing each other around the backyard.

"I suddenly want a dog," Shelley exclaimed, and Rand laughed with her. "I've really never been around them before."

"That is the saddest thing I've ever heard," Rachel said as she came to the sliding glass door in a T-shirt over her bathing suit. Wet spots were beginning to form in random places where it touched her. "Rachel Grady, and you're Shelley Whitmore." She then said, "Did you get my Diet Coke yet?"

"Oh," Jamie said, then turned back to the fridge, pulled one out, and turned. "Catch," she said, looking at Rachel.

"Don't you dare," Rachel warned her, but it was too late. The can sailed through the air toward her, and Rand reached up and caught it. She set it down on the counter, and Jamie took another from the fridge and walked slowly to hand it to Rand to reach to Rachel, who took it with a look of disgust on her face and sat outside at the table.

"These are my best friends," Rand told Shelley. "I've known them since I was seventeen and they won't leave me alone."

"I think they're wonderful," Shelley said.

CHAPTER TEN

Rachel, Jamie, Rand, and Shelley sat in cushioned chairs on the patio. The dogs settled and Jackson chose to sit next to Rachel, while June sat by Shelley. Rand watched Shelley touch June's ears like they were a miracle. Rand pulled a face when Rachel nudged Jamie with her foot.

"Shelley is going to help with my lawsuit," Rand said, interrupting the silence.

"You are?" Rachel asked, her hair was drying, natural curls standing up in random places on her head. She crossed her legs like she was wearing a thousand-dollar dress and pearls and sipped her Diet Coke.

"I offered, yes. I came to get the previous paperwork." Shelley looked up from June but kept her hand on her.

"What are you thinking?" Rachel's gaze was direct.

"I'm going to countersue them. Make a tort claim," Shelley said succinctly, directly. "I mean, it probably won't have a ton of merit, neither does their claim, but I think it will scare them off. I don't think they'll get someone to sue again after this. They'll look vexatious."

"Vex-a what, who, yeah," Jamie said.

"My sentiments exactly," Rachel said.

"And she's the smart one," Jamie said, pointing at Rachel, who raised her eyebrows.

"Vexatious litigants are people who abuse the legal system for harassment purposes. The court doesn't appreciate misuse. There are laws against it. Based on what you told me, I'm surprised they could find a lawyer to sue you. Usually, vexatious litigants represent themselves." Shelley paused and turned to look at Rand, who listened to her intently. "In your case, I believe Kim's parents are using the legal system to harass you, and I intend to build a civil tort claim against them, on your behalf. I don't think their claims have merit, but I'll look at the lawsuit. Regardless, a countersuit should shock them awake."

"Did you pass the bar here?" Rand looked at Rachel as she finished the question. It hadn't occurred to Rand to ask that.

"Yes," Shelley said. "Given the work I've done politically, I'm licensed in a number of states."

Rachel held out her fist across the small table between them. Shelley tipped her head, and Jamie interpreted. "Fist bump."

Shelley smiled and reached to bump Rachel's fist, her first such fist bump. "I think you'll find that I'm, um…" Shelley hesitated. "I'm not sure how to word it. So, I'll just be honest and say socially awkward, so help is always appreciated."

Rachel smiled, approval written all over her face. "I like you. You can hang out with us anytime." Shelley smiled but seemed embarrassed and concentrated on the dog. Rand put her feet up on the table, folding her arms across her middle, watching Shelley from the corner of her eyes.

"You're going to sue them back?" Jamie clarified. "Is that what I understand?"

"That's exactly what I'm going to do." Shelley was resolved, with quiet, unassuming strength, and then she smiled. "I mean, most of it is really just posturing. But posturing works. Unfortunately, sometimes it's necessary to hit back. With Rand's approval, of course."

Rand's focus drifted from Jamie and Rachel to Shelley as she considered the course of action carefully. She had no desire to engage so directly with Kim's parents, but she also wanted it to end. The lawsuit left her feeling desperate and hollow in a way she couldn't even articulate to Mary. Perhaps this course of action would break the cycle they were locked in and allow all of them to move forward.

"Yes," Rand said before she could overthink. "I need it to stop. I can't take it anymore." Shelley nodded reassuringly, and for the first time in years, Rand struck back against the winged monster of grief in her chest and glimpsed the possibility of letting it go.

After everyone left her house, Rand slipped her wedding ring off and slid it into a small case in the top drawer of her dresser. She stood in front of the drawer, breathing through the urge to put it back on. As it passed, she climbed into the bed never shared with anyone and looked at the light filtering through the blinds on the window. She was overcome with a sensation of aloneness. She was in a house, all by herself. She'd felt the presence of Kim's ghost for so long the awareness rose with fear and panic.

She rolled onto her back, looked at the ceiling, thought about the arc of her life, and admitted she'd lost the last few years. She remembered very little of her days except getting into her car and driving to work. Rand asked Mary constantly to determine her fitness to see patients and was reassured by the support. Since Kim died, her memories came back to her in black and white, tinged with deadness.

Grief, she thought. It seeped into every crevice of her being, without her conscious participation, and while there, overwrote her better self like a computer virus. Grief compounded, fed itself, re-created itself until she invited it into embrace, saw it for what it was—lost love. The only memory of the past few years that greeted her with color and warmth was Shelley in Manhattan and her daily emails.

Rand rolled back to her side, pulled her legs up to her chest, and held them at the knees. She loved Shelley's emails. She marveled at her use of language, felt space open up inside of her when a message appeared in the email inbox. Now she was here, in person, willing to help her move forward. She sat downstairs on her patio, talked to her friends, and laughed at Jamie's jokes. Rand liked her laugh and watched her breasts move when she did, though she'd never admit this out loud. Was it objectifying, she wondered, to like looking at someone's breasts so much?

Shelley had changed her hair since she saw her in Manhattan. Rand liked it. She thought about Shelley and drifted to sleep in a flash, wishing she was next to her in bed. Kim left, Rand thought, confused as sleep came, and Shelley was there.

CHAPTER ELEVEN

Shelley returned home from Target, carrying three bags and a standing tower fan. Since returning home the night before from Rand's, she was consumed by lawsuits and researching precedents. By late afternoon, she needed a change of scenery and went to Target. She was putting groceries away when excruciating pain in her side doubled her over.

Hand on the counter, she gasped, alarmed and terrified. Another cramp took her to her knees, and she fought for breath as pain exploded in her abdomen. A flash of heat ran up her side and spread across her chest, raced up her neck, and set her head on fire. She found the will to push up from one knee. Her goal was her cell phone on the television stand. She stumbled and knocked it behind the stand. She cried out, fell to both knees, more pain across her abdomen, which left her momentarily unable to move.

Prone on the ground, she yanked the television stand forward, her last desperate attempt to survive. The phone was solid against her fingertips and felt like hope. She dialed 9-1-1. "Help me," she said while darkness formed around her field of vision.

"Can you tell me your name? Where are you?" Shelley mumbled her address, surprised to know it already and looked up at the door handle. "Are you alone?" the 9-1-1 operator asked.

"Yes," Shelley said with a cry. "I don't know what's wrong. I have pain across my abdomen and I'm losing consciousness," Shelley said in a moment of rational clarity. "I'm alone in my apartment and the door is unlocked." She let go of the phone, and it rolled from her hand, falling once again behind the television stand. Then there was darkness.

❖

Shelley was just alert enough to remember a paramedic bending over her. "We're here," she said, "We've got you." The ride to the hospital was a blur. She regained consciousness under a bright exam light. Someone cut off her shirt and there was cold steel against her leg.

"She's awake," a female said. Shelley struggled to follow the voice, tried to move. Then there was a firm hand on her shoulder and another voice spoke. One she recognized.

"Shelley, it's me. It's Rachel. Do you know where you are?" Rachel's form steadied and Shelley fought to focus and hold on to control. She tried to speak, but nothing came out of her mouth. "You're in the hospital. The paramedics brought you here. Your appendix ruptured, so you're on your way to emergency surgery, okay? Do you want me to call Rand?"

"Yes," Shelley whispered. "Am I going to die?"

"No, you're not. I'll be there when you wake up. We're going to put you to sleep now, okay? I've got you." She was suddenly aware of an IV in her hand. She watched someone in scrubs inject something and fixed her gaze on Rachel as the world went black again.

CHAPTER TWELVE

When Rachel called, Rand's heartbeat nearly drowned out every other sound in the world. She called Jamie in a panic on her way to the hospital. That something might happen to Shelley sent shockwaves through her insides, dislodging the icebergs that formed the past few years. Jamie arrived just as she sat down and began obsessively checking her phone for updates from Rachel.

"You are so freaked out," Jamie said, touching Rand's shoulder. "Rachel said she'll be okay, so she'll be okay. Try to calm down."

"Do you know how wrong it is to tell someone to calm down when they're upset?"

"You're the therapist, not me, so calm down," Jamie said again. "You're making me all agitated and I didn't stop at the dispensary."

"You're self-medicating with pot," Rand said, suddenly disengaged from worry about Shelley.

"No, I'm not. I got a doctor's signature. So technically, it's a prescription."

"You know very well what I'm saying. I could get you in with someone who could give you an FDA approved pharmaceutical for your moods," Rand said.

"Oh my God. A drug is a drug and cannabis is au naturel. I'd rather use it than something made in a factory."

At that moment, the swinging doors opened and Rachel came toward them. Rand met her in the middle of the room. Rachel tugged her arm and led her to the chairs.

"I need to sit," she said. "She's fine, Rand. We got to her soon enough. They cleaned her abdominal cavity really well, and she's on the strongest antibiotics on the planet. She's going to be here a week or so, though."

"Can I visit her?" Rand perched on the edge of the seat.

"When she wakes up," Rachel said. "I asked the attending nurse to let you know her room number."

"Did you do the surgery?" Rand shifted, anxious.

"No," Rachel said. "I know her. And someone else was available. But I popped in and watched."

"You look so tired," Jamie said to Rachel.

"I am." Rachel rested her head against the wall and shut her eyes. "I am going to go lie down for an hour. I need to take out a gallbladder before I go home, but I can't do it without some rest. I'll come check on Shelley later." Rand hugged her, grateful, and Jamie stood as Rachel walked away from them, the double doors swinging closed behind her.

Jamie turned to Rand. "That looked pretty cool, right?"

"Like a scene from ER," Rand said. "Go home. I'll wait to see her, see what she needs. The beagles will be anxious."

"Do you like her?" Jamie put her hand on Rand's shoulder.

"She's brilliant and kind. She's surprising." Rand looked at Jamie from the corner of her eyes.

"Pretty too," Jamie said, finger up. Rand agreed silently with a small smile.

"I haven't, except Kim, you know. And with all this, it's probably best I don't right now. Not the healthiest thing, since she's helping me resolve it."

"Hmm." Nothing more. "Well," Jamie said, "I'll leave you to your rationalizations then. Call if you need something." She kissed Rand's head as she stood. As she walked away, she yelled, over her shoulder, "You like her!" Jamie ran through the automatic doors laughing, and Rand watched her run down the sidewalk only to stop on the other side of the window. She mouthed, "You like her. You wanna kiss her." She made a kissy face and then waved and sauntered across the parking lot like the whole world belonged to her.

CHAPTER THIRTEEN

S helley returned to consciousness with two drip bags attached to an IV in her arm. Rand waited in the doorway, as if unwilling to violate her privacy.

"May I come in?" Shelley tried to sit up. "Don't do that," Rand said, coming to her side. "Just rest. I'll just sit here with you, if that's okay."

"You don't need to," Shelley said. "Now that Rachel saved me."

"That's what she does. Saves people." The setting sun cast a deep orange light into the small, beige room. Shelley's heart rate monitors beeped, and the chair crackled under Rand's weight. "If you'd like to be alone, I can leave. But I have nowhere else to be tonight, so I can sit with you."

Shelley's head was heavy, and she was vaguely aware of the incision on her side. The memory of falling into unconsciousness by herself was not far from her mind, and a deep well of panic welled up in her. With the pain meds and leftover anesthesia, Shelley's coping mechanisms had curled up and gone to bed.

There was nothing meaningful around her to count, and she was too tired to reframe her experience. Instead, she looked at Rand and said, "It was really scary." Then, she told her what happened, how the phone slipped away behind the stand, relief at seeing the door handle unlocked, and waking to paramedics standing in her apartment.

Rand took her hand, silent, listening. Her fingers slipped between Shelley's, without any thought, and Rand covered their entwined hands with her other. "I'm so glad you were able to get help." Shelley closed her eyes. "How long do you have to stay?"

"Through Friday morning, at least," a voice behind her answered.

Rachel was there. Rand turned to look at her, letting go of Shelley's hand, suddenly conscious she'd taken it. Rachel walked to Shelley's IV drip and checked it. Then she looked at the line in Shelley's arm. "How do you feel? Is your pain okay?"

"I can feel my side, in tingles and bursts."

"The nerve block will continue to wear off like that. If it begins to hurt too much, let the nurses know and we can give you a pain med, okay?" Rachel then reached up to the small computer next to Shelley's bed and typed one-handed. She held a prefilled syringe in her other hand. "I'm going to give you something right now, okay? It's going to make you sleepy. Don't fight it." Rachel injected the medication in Shelley's IV. "That was really close, Shelley. Another ten minutes and I don't even want to think about it. We got you cleaned out really well, but you have to stay here so we can monitor the infection. Keep you on antibiotics. She pointed to one of the bags. "Did you have any symptoms before this?"

"I did. Now I realize what it was. The past few weeks," Shelley said. "I can't imagine what would have happened if I'd been on my road trip. I should be happy it waited on my arrival here."

"Most people miss the symptoms leading up to appendicitis. But it's out now. You don't need it anyway." Rachel smiled at her.

"I thought you had a gallbladder to remove," Rand said.

"They got someone else. So, I came up here and I am going home now to sleep for two days straight."

"Assuming Jamie leaves you alone," Rand said.

"Can you entertain her?" Rachel laughed and touched Shelley's arm. Her touch was earnest, gentle, and firm. Shelley felt comforted and trusted her. "Rest. You can go home in a few days. We just need to make sure the infection is under control."

"Thank you," Shelley said, and Rachel rubbed her arm and gave it a gentle squeeze as she turned to walk away.

"Don't keep her awake," she said to Rand, who saluted her.

"Do you want me to leave so you can sleep?"

"No," Shelley said. "I mean, if you don't mind. I don't want to be alone right away. Which is strange, because I usually always want to be alone, but I find I don't right now." Rand's eyes were kind and Shelley wanted her to hold her hand again, but Rand sat back in the chair next to the bed, hands crossed in her lap. Shelley stared at them and wondered how they would feel on her skin after pulling off her shirt. She tore her gaze away, mustering enough control not to fantasize about Rand while she was hooked up to IV drips.

They drifted into comfortable silence, and Shelley felt the medicine Rachel gave her as it spread through her body. The sharp pain in her abdomen faded with the detailed edges of her vision. Panic rose from her knees as she felt her loss of control. Shelley struggled against it letting out a tiny cry as she slipped toward unconsciousness. But then Rand's hand was on her arm. She heard, "It's okay. It's the medicine Rachel gave you. You're safe. I'm going to stay right here." Shelley reached for Rand's hand, who seemed happy to acquiesce.

With Rand close, Shelley murmured, drifting to sleep, "I like you so much."

"Me too you," Rand said as Shelley's eyes closed.

❖

Shelley woke hours later and looked to the right, where Rand was before. The chair was empty, and distress welled inside her. The clock said it was midnight. The door to the room was closed, but noise from the hallway filtered in, in the crack on the floor. Voices called out for help, and carts clanked. Other doors slammed. She closed her eyes, more alert and focused than earlier, when she heard water from the left. She turned as the bathroom door opened. Rand walked out, and upon seeing her eyes open, smiled.

"There you are," she said, coming around the bed to stand next to the right side again.

"It's so late," Shelley said with a glance at the clock. "Go home."

"I didn't want to leave while you were sleeping."

Shelley felt her words in her chest like tiny fireworks bursting over a lake at summer's end. There were not enough words to describe how Rand made her feel. She didn't know how to respond and was overwhelmed by the sensations in her body.

"How are you? Do you need anything?" Rand spoke again.

"Water, I think."

"The nurse brought some when you were sleeping. Said you could have some." She poured it for Shelley, and then scooted the rolling table toward her, leaving the cup on it.

Shelley held the bed control. "Wish me luck." She moved slowly up and grimaced as her body bent. More inclined, she took a sip of water. Then, insecure about how she looked, Shelley pulled the elastic in her hair free, shook it loose, and pulled it back up. The gown she wore was atrocious and she wanted to crawl under the blankets and hide.

"I can come back in the morning. If you give me your address, I can stop and get some clothes for you. Anything else you need. Since you're going to be here a while," Rand said.

"You've already done too much. I don't want to inconvenience you more."

"Stop," Rand said. "Let me help. I want to help. You can even stay a few days in my guest bedroom if you'd like, when you're done. You don't need to decide now. See how you feel." Shelley was more self-conscious in that moment than she'd ever remembered. "Do you need help getting back down?"

"I'm going to sit up for a bit, I think." Shelley mustered all her strength to hold eye contact. "Maybe my laptop and phone with their chargers?"

"Sure," Rand said. "Anything else?"

"Some clothes for when I go home," Shelley said. "And my hotspot. It's on top of my laptop."

"I don't think the Wi-Fi here is very good," Rand said, holding up her phone. "I tried to stream a show last night and nothing would come through."

"I can't go a week without Netflix," Shelley said.

"Introverted coping mechanisms," Rand said, and Shelley laughed. "Hotspot it is. Healing is holistic."

"Thank you," Shelley said, once again uncomfortable with Rand's help. She hated feeling like a burden.

"It's my pleasure," Rand said. "Okay, then, tomorrow morning. Sleep. I'll be back with gifts."

Shelley wanted to say, "Don't go," but instead said, "Thank you so much for staying with me. For being so kind."

"I'll be back in the morning, okay?" Then Rand turned to leave, a single glance back over her shoulder as Shelley raised her hand to her. The door shut quietly, but the momentary glimpse of bright light in the hall left spots in Shelley's eyes. She rested her head against the pillow, felt a sharp stab of pain in her side, and closed her eyes, unsettled and uncomfortable.

She wanted to stand and use the bathroom but was afraid to do so herself, so she pressed the nurse call button and waited patiently, thinking about her near miss as the phone fell behind the television stand, Rachel, and then Rand, sitting next to her until after midnight. She waited for her to wake up.

Something had come to life inside her a year ago, and as it grew, all sorts of hidden tendrils of energy exploded at random intervals of her life. She was living in a psychological minefield, creeping slowly outward where she kept encountering her own shadow projections. Each explosive event stripped away another layer of her hesitation, as though the Finger of God had touched her life, and now she had no choice but to awaken to her truth. The door opened and the nurse appeared, as Shelley's next steps became abundantly clear.

CHAPTER FOURTEEN

Rand stared at Shelley's dresser. She'd collected her laptop, phone, and hotspot and found her keys on the floor. It was all easy in comparison to riffling through her underwear. What kind of underwear did Shelley wear? Did she call them "panties"? Rand bet she called them panties. Rand covered her eyes with her hand and yanked the drawer open. She'd have to look. How else would she know it wasn't a sock in her hand?

Shelley folded her underwear in neat rows. There were tiny little square blobs of fabric, indistinct in shape and make. If Rand could lift the underwear gingerly from the drawer, Shelley's underthings would remain a mystery to her and wouldn't be top of mind when they saw each other at the hospital. Rand lifted a few pairs, with two bras, and quickly shoved them into a gym bag from the top shelf in Shelley's closet.

The bedroom was sparsely decorated, but still warm somehow. Shelley had a richly textured quilt on the bed and three full bookcases. Rand perused the titles. Legal books. History books. Books about religion and spirituality. Rand recognized some as recommendations they'd discussed via email. Books by Karin Kallmaker and Radcylffe. Rand picked one up. Shelley had read it, the seam was bent and well worn.

Shelley was aware of her sexuality. Rand put the book back on the shelf, ashamed to intrude on Shelley's privacy. Did it matter she was reading lesbian romances? It did, Rand thought. It mattered that Shelley replied to her emails almost immediately. It mattered that she'd taken a job in Phoenix, when there were likely many options for relocation. It mattered that she'd left her life to begin again after the picture of her surfaced. Rand didn't know if she should ask her about it.

They'd only ever spent the one night together, in New York, and their coffee date the day before. Their ongoing correspondence had buoyed their intimacy and created a deeper connection than what was manifest in the physical world. Was the connection she felt based on assumed intimacy? Would Shelley come out of the closet and be open about who she was? Or would she keep it tucked away forever? If she wanted Rand, what kind of relationship would she expect?

Rand knew she wouldn't accept anything less than an open relationship. The whole world needed to know. It was one thing to keep a couple of romances tucked on your shelf and another thing entirely to be out, open, and proud. That was a relationship requirement for her. Was Shelley capable of that? And if she was, did Rand want her?

Rand situated Shelley's things in the bag and scanned the small apartment to make sure nothing was missing from her mental inventory. Shelley's iPad was on the table, so Rand grabbed it too. She checked to make sure the balcony door was locked, and then left, locking up.

Rand descended the steep stairs, bag on her shoulder. She liked Shelley and was attracted to her. She couldn't stop talking to her even when her instincts told her to flee. Was it all some subconscious projection of guilt? Falling for an unattainable, closeted, gay Republican? Rand laughed out loud as she slid into the driver's seat of the car. If it was a subconscious projection, it was a doozy. She'd outdone herself this time.

❖

Rand delivered Shelley's belongings. Shelley had washed her face and changed her hospital gown. Her hair was brushed and fell in long waves around her face. There was a toothbrush on the counter by the sink.

"You look ready to hit the town," Rand said, teasing her as Shelley lifted her laptop from the computer bag.

"See, now, I know you're just playing with me." Rand grinned, silent. "Thanks for getting all this. I hope it wasn't too awkward."

Rand thought about the moment in front of her dresser. It was, but she wouldn't tell her. Instead, she said, "You have an amazing library. I glanced. I hope you don't mind."

"No, not at all. Feel free to borrow anything you'd like," Shelley said. "I saw your bookcases when I was over and was just too shy to ask to browse. It's like a trip to the library."

Rand thought about saying something about the lesbian books, then decided not to approach the topic. Shelley could, if she wanted.

"How do you feel? Do you want to rest, or could you use some company?"

"Your company would be wonderful," Shelley said. "I can already tell I'm going to be bored here."

"But this is nothing to take chances with," Rand said.

"I know," Shelley said. "The past year or so has been relentless. One thing after another. One change after another. I think it's something I'm doing."

"It's because you want to change," Rand said, scooting closer to the bed. "I see it all the time with patients. You told me in New York, and via email, that something is going on with you." Shelley looked directly at Rand. Rand stopped talking and gazed at the rich brown of her eyes. Her skin was flushed and clean, unblemished, young. Shelley didn't look like she'd turned the corner into thirty.

"Yes," Shelley said, prompting Rand.

"Oh, yeah," Rand said, back to attention. She was gazing into the dreamy eyes of a gay Republican. "It's like your conscious world has to get your subconscious world caught up. The universe has a terrible, vindictive sense of humor, saying, 'Oh, you think you're ready for change? You think you're ready to be who you are? Can you take this?' There is research about quantum consciousness you might find interesting. I'll bring the book for you tomorrow. About how our preconditioned subconscious minds secretly sabotage us when we begin operating with higher intentions." Shelley watched her but said nothing. "What?"

"Oh, I didn't know if you were done. I think I just wanted you to keep talking," Shelley said, and then immediately blushed.

"Think about your desire to change like a muscle you need to work out," Rand said. She was thrilled Shelley wanted to listen. "The universe is going to make you work for what you want. Makes you reorganize your relationship with reality. Or so I like to think it works that way."

"That's really poignant," Shelley said. "I love your words. I watched some of your videos."

"You did?" Rand was surprised.

"I did. I don't think I really understood transgender rights before I met you that day. You made me connect to it viscerally. I think you have a gift with words."

"Well, does this mean you're going to update your voter registration to be a Democrat?" Rand smiled.

"No," Shelley said. "Not because I don't like you, but because I don't like large, intrusive government. I like personal liberty."

"That's dramatic," Rand said. "Not all government is intrusive."

"I like space for entrepreneurs to create, people to move freely without state interference or undue tax burden. I believe in states' rights and that the federal government is not our savior. It's just an institution like any other, and generally, I've come to understand I don't like institutions," Shelley said. "We talked about that the other day. Corporations are their own evil, aren't they? Left unchecked. I'm still not sure what the answer is. But I'll listen. To you."

"I have an important duty on behalf of all gay, liberal kind," Rand said.

"Maybe," Shelley said. "I think there's ample opportunity for the Republican Party to extract themselves from culture wars and focus on personal liberty. You can't simultaneously argue against economic regulation while wanting to enforce Judeo-Christian religious beliefs."

"I can't get past that," Rand said. "I don't know how any self-respecting gay person could."

"Polls show that forty-four percent of Republicans favor gay marriage, Rand. You're focused on the Evangelical portion of the party."

"No, I'm focused on the party's platform that says marriage is between a man and a woman. They do that to keep that portion of the voter bloc in place, and it has real world ramifications."

"I can't argue with that," Shelley said.

"Imagine how amazing this conversation would be if you'd hadn't just had major surgery," Rand said, surprised by Shelley's response. Shelley laughed. "How did we go from quantum consciousness to personal liberty?"

"Maybe it's just what we do," Shelley said. They fell silent. "Do you think my subconscious is about caught up with my conscious mind? Because I'm tired."

"It depends," Rand said.

"On what?"

"What comes next. What you decide you want," Rand said.

"I'm scared," Shelley said. "Not because I nearly died. Because I've wanted to die, at many different points in my life."

Rand grabbed her hand, alarmed. "You're not—"

"No, I'm not suicidal," Shelley said. "It's just, what do you do when you let go of everything you've ever known?" The question struck so close to Rand, tears rolled down her face. "Rand, I didn't mean to upset you. Of course, you would know."

"I'm just really emotional. You didn't do anything wrong. The thing is, I don't know what you do. I've been trying to figure it out too."

"Maybe we can help each other," Shelley said. Her gaze was so innocent and open Rand felt guilty for thinking of her as a gay Republican. She deserved so much more from her.

"It's a deal," Rand said.

The nurse interrupted them then to change Shelley's IV bag. Rand kept her gaze on Shelley, whose attention the nurse commandeered.

Rand thought about the countless emails they'd exchanged since they met in Manhattan the year before. She knew what kind of bike Shelley rode in junior high, where she'd hide from her father and read books of poetry from the library. How she snuck snacks into her bedroom, her mother openly critical of her weight. Shelley met her eyes and smiled, and Rand felt comfortable and safe and attributed it to their long correspondence. But she was also aware enough to know that she'd opened herself to Shelley. In those same emails, she shared details of her childhood, stories about her parents and their eccentric friends, and her struggles with depression.

Now, with Shelley in Phoenix, just across from her, Rand understood the risks viscerally for the first time. What if Shelley fell in love with her and it didn't work out? What if she wasn't ready to get involved with someone so seriously and their breakup harmed Shelley, who despite her brilliance, was deeply sensitive? Rachel had told her a few months before that her over-preoccupation with care for others was both endearing and egotistical, and Rand remembered this as she slipped into the corner of the room to allow the nurse space.

CHAPTER FIFTEEN

By day two in the hospital, Shelley was restless and desperate. She liked to be still, but stillness in a hospital was a myth. Her sleep was constantly interrupted by nurses checking her temperature and medication. Her mother and father called when she texted to tell them what happened and offered to fly to Phoenix to help her recover. It was a generous offer, but she assured them it was fine. She'd recover in the hospital and only be released when it was safe. All of her siblings reached out for the first time since the picture.

The next day, a courier brought a box of books from her dad with a handwritten note that he expected her to call after she read them to discuss. A canister of her favorite homemade cookies came from her mom. She cried at their thoughtfulness and love, even if it was imperfect. Rand found her that way.

"It's confusing," Rand told her. "How much damage the people who love us can do to us without knowing it."

"It's weird to be human," Shelley said. She held the cookie tin out to Rand. "Take one. They're vegan. And delicious. Chocolate and coconut."

Shelley left the hospital and went home with Rand to stay the night in her guest room. She was afraid to be alone and told Rand so, who looked at her with appreciation. "That was brave," Rand said. "To admit you don't want to be alone."

Shelley slept soundly for the rest of the day, feeling only mildly self-conscious about it. When she woke about six p.m., there was a clean towel and her bag of clothes in the small bathroom. Shelley showered and washed her hair, resting against the tub wall as the water ran over her. She lathered her hair with Rand's shampoo, an eco-friendly brand, not tested on animals, and smiled as she held the bottle in her hand.

She dried with the towel Rand left her, and held it up to her face and smelled the detergent. Shelley put on lotion and clothes, her abdomen sore but healing. She towel dried her hair and then dug around in the bag for something to use to tie it back. She opened the bathroom door and paused to lean against the wall. Shelley took a deep breath, wanting certainty her legs were steady enough to walk.

She heard movement in the kitchen and moved tentatively down the hallway before pausing at the entry. Rand wore a pair of jeans and a T-shirt and was barefoot at the counter. A small television on the counter was on MSNBC. Shelley watched Rand cut watermelon for a few moments. Finally, as Rand turned toward the fridge, Shelley said, "Hi."

Rand responded with an excited smile, dropped her hands from the air where she'd moved to open the fridge, and moved toward Shelley. "You're awake," Rand said. She put her hands on Shelley's hips gently. Shelley grabbed Rand's elbows. The ease of the greeting thrilled Shelley. Rand took her hands from Shelley's hips with a shy smile and went to the fridge. Shelley followed her, touching her hips where Rand's hands had been.

"I'm making dinner. I was hoping you'd wake. I've got lentils on the stove, asparagus in the oven, and rice cooking. Watermelon because, well, watermelon." Rand lifted the bowl of watermelon to the table and handed Shelley a fork. She prepared a plate and set it in front of Shelley.

"Can I get you something to drink?"

"Water would be amazing," Shelley said, covering her mouth as she chewed the watermelon.

"Ice?" Rand asked as she lifted a glass from the cupboard, and Shelley nodded, mouth full.

"I despise room temperature water," Shelley said after swallowing the watermelon. "It's insulting. I feel like civilization is made possible by ice and central air. Otherwise, it's the Middle Ages."

"Or Alabama?" Rand asked with a smile.

"Ouch." Shelley laughed.

"Sorry," Rand said.

"I'm from Georgia," Shelley said. "So, you know, close but not a direct shot across my bow. You Democrats can be pretty intolerant." She was only partially teasing.

"Touché," Rand said, hands in the air. "How do you feel?"

"I'm sore, but I don't feel like I'm going to die anymore. Thank you for dinner," she said. MSNBC covered Trump's latest Tweets, and a commentator derided the Republican Party. "Does it bother you that I'm conservative?" Shelley asked as she took her first bite. "Oh my God, this is delicious. Are these red lentils?"

"Yes," Rand said, and then corrected herself. "Yes, to red lentils, no, to conservative. At least, I don't think so. I'm absolutely not. Evolution is natural." She turned off the television and joined Shelley at the table.

Shelley ate, took a drink, and sat quietly. "It doesn't bother me that you're liberal. I understand your perspective. But I don't think laissez-faire economics precludes a capacity to evolve."

"Tell your base that," Rand said.

"I don't disagree. But can't that be challenged from within?"

"But it's not being challenged. I'm not much of an incrementalist," Rand said. "More of an activist."

"I'm pretty pragmatic," Shelley said. But not about Rand. There was nothing pragmatic about how she felt for Rand. Shelley scooted the chair, like she was getting more food.

"Let me," Rand said, quickly taking the plate. "I'm glad you liked it." She refilled her plate and glass and returned it to her.

"You're liberal, but still traditional in so many ways," Shelley observed. "You're not like Jamie."

"Who is?" Rand laughed.

"Am I keeping you from anything?"

"No," Rand reassured her. "I was just wondering if you feel like sitting up to watch some television or if you'd rather go back to bed."

"I think I'd like to be up for a while," Shelley said. "I can go home too. I'm better."

"Why don't you stay one more night? Just to be sure?" Shelley agreed, relieved. She didn't want to be alone, but also wanted to be with Rand more than anything else. Rand cleaned up while Shelley talked about a book she was reading, a little nervous and unsteady. If Rand noticed, she just didn't say anything. Shelley watched her clean up. When she was finished, she held out her hand to Shelley, who took it, and they walked into the front room together. Rand helped Shelley settle on the small sofa and then sat down next to her with the remote in her hand.

They settled on a movie and Shelley wished Rand would put her arm around her, let her curl up against her, but she didn't. Instead, Rand put her feet up on the ottoman, next to Shelley's and folded her arms across her chest and relaxed into her corner of the couch. Shelley sighed, adjusted, and leaned her foot against Rand's, then fell asleep on the couch until Rand roused her to crawl into bed an hour or so later.

CHAPTER SIXTEEN

Rand took Shelley home on her way to work, imploring her to call if she needed anything. Shelley called her boss and planned to work from home for a few days to continue to recover. She had a blog article due about sales tax and civic responsibility, and it was something she could write without a lot of energy or thought. During the following days, in her solitude, interrupted by visits from Rand, Rachel, and an amazing one from Jamie and the beagles, she focused on her work, the lawsuit, and her plan for redemption.

It was redemption that occupied the most of her consciousness during these long days, with a dull ache in her side, where a part of her was cut out. She'd spent the first thirty-one years of her life in service of her father's quest, sublimating her needs and deepest desires. In that path, she'd worked against her own best interests. Shelley never consulted on cases about gay marriage, silently abdicating the chore to others in her circle, but acquiescence to her father's social conservatism and Evangelicalism was its own burden to shed.

When she finally healed, she went to work and sat down in front of Nate and told him, "I'm gay. I'm going to come out. I need to know if that is going to be an issue."

Nate sat back, hands on his large stomach, eyes wide. He lifted one hand to wipe the sweat on top of his balding head, and pressed stray hairs down. "Really?" he asked, incredulous. "I mean, you're a lesbian?" Shelley laughed then and leaned forward, nodding. "Wow." He stared at her. "I mean I saw the picture, but you didn't say anything, so I didn't pursue it."

"Is this going to be a problem?" She crossed her legs.

"No—I mean, no. I want the story on our site first, though. That's the deal. The major news outlets can pick it up from us."

"Okay," she agreed. "But," she held up a finger, "I have one condition."

"Yeah?" Someone laughed in the background and a chair fell. Neither one of them turned to look.

"No more anti-gay pandering. We don't run articles that marginalize and exclude. We don't let Christians make themselves the victims of the gay rights movement, because you and I both know they are not."

"I don't run many of those anyway," Nate said defensively. "I want to focus on policy, not cultural wars."

"I've seen a couple over the years. You stay the true, late life Barry Goldwater, Libertarian course, let people be who they are, without interference, stay completely out of culture wars. I'll do this and stay with you if you promise we never become Breitbart."

"Don't become some socialist lefty," he said and stuck out his hand. Shelley shook it.

"I'll get the article ready. MSNBC invited me back mid-June. Let's plan to post it when I get back."

"Not a word. To anyone, got it? It's our exclusive."

"You realize this is my life, right?"

"That's all any of this is. Someone's life. This is going to drive up our subscriber base." She agreed. "Are you telling your family first?" Nate suddenly asked, less excited, more focused on her, a hint of concern in his watery, red eyes. He drank a lot of coffee, Shelley had noticed, and didn't sleep much.

"No," she said. She didn't know what else to say, so she uncrossed her legs, then crossed them again. Nate waited, looking at her. "It wouldn't matter. They already know. I tried to share, but they didn't want to hear it."

"What about your faith?"

"I don't spend my days talking to God, if that's what you're wondering." Nate just looked at her. "Evangelicalism belongs to my father, not me. I think it's a psychological condition when taken to the extreme. Want me to write an article about that?" She laughed and he relaxed, the tension releasing.

"Yeah, actually. Next. Okay, well, just don't underestimate this. I know you almost died, so," he said, not finishing his thought.

"Oh, you think I'm doing this because I almost died alone in my apartment with a ruptured appendix?"

"Yeah," he said.

"It's been building for quite a while. That might have jarred me even further awake, but why do you think I finally took your job offer?" Nate stared at an unfixed location behind her head. "So, we're good? Give me until the first of June and I'll get the article done." She stood to leave his office.

"Shelley," he said, and she paused at the door. "This is brave." She smiled, pleased she'd heard that a lot lately. She worked at her desk for a few hours, sent off her article, and then left for the day. The late afternoon sun was suffocating, but she felt better than she had for weeks. She decided to call Rand. She didn't text. She called.

For Shelley, the boldness of the choice could not be underestimated. But then, once she dialed and waited by the car door to let the heat dissipate some before climbing inside, her heart hammered in her chest. What if Rand didn't answer?

Her fear wasn't warranted because Rand did, after just two rings. Shelley heard her voice and smiled, then remembered to speak. "What are you doing tonight?"

"Nothing," Rand said. "I just finished up at the office and am going home."

"There is a food truck event in Peoria. Would you come with me?" Co-workers discussed it earlier in the day, and she overheard.

There was a pause on the other side of the phone, and Shelley felt it with trepidation. But then she released her breath when Rand answered, "Yes. What time?"

Shelley was content to let Rand drive. She came to her apartment and Shelley sat in the front seat with one bare foot tucked under her, flip-flops waiting on the car mat below. They'd crossed to Peoria on surface streets, avoiding the busy freeways, and Shelley watched unfamiliar areas of the city unfold.

She wished there were more colors to the city, but it was her only complaint. Otherwise, she liked the dry air, the wide streets, the impeccable, organized infrastructure. On the East Coast and in Atlanta, the streets felt laborious, difficult to navigate, but in Phoenix she felt as if she moved with greater ease. She focused her attention on Rand.

"How are you?" she asked. "I've been so consumed by my own issues, I'm not sure I've checked in with you."

"You're fine. I'm okay. A bit tired, to be honest."

"Too tired to go?"

"God, no," Rand said. "I perked up when you called." Shelley flushed and waited silently for more information.

None was forthcoming so she spoke. "I've drafted your countersuit." Rand sat quietly, driving. "It's pretty scathing. Emotional distress. And so on." Rand smiled but still said nothing. Her posture stiffened, and Shelley noted the change in the energy between them. "Rand, I won't do anything without your consent." Rand acknowledged her with a thumbs-up but still said nothing. "What they're doing isn't fair, ethical, or right."

"I know," Rand said, shifting in the driver's seat as if she wanted to flee. Shelley thought if they'd been on land, Rand would have run. She imagined chasing her across a parking lot into a busy intersection. "It's just that, well..." she hesitated and shook her head.

"It feels gross," Shelley answered for her. "I know. We can explore different options. I mean, I can represent you. We reach out to their attorney. I tell them that if they don't drop the suit, we'll countersue. Before I actually do it..." Shelley trailed off, waiting for a reaction.

"Can I think on it?" Shelley watched Rand's hands on the steering wheel, how her knuckles slanted with delicate strength. Her forearms were thin but strong too, and Shelley's gaze traveled up to her profile. The sun caught the gray in her hair, and Shelley flushed with desire. She wanted to touch her and instead pulled her gaze away.

"You can do whatever you need to do. Just let me know. You can bring it up next time, okay? It's your show."

CHAPTER SEVENTEEN

They'd parked at the food truck event. Rand stood at the end of the car waiting for Shelley. Her instinct was to take her hand, but she hesitated, uncertain. She looked down at Shelley's hand as they began to walk together and felt adolescent. Rand wanted to grab her hand in Manhattan too. The wind picked up as they stood in line for the entrance, and by the time they'd paid their five dollars, a thunderclap rang through the sky, and a burst of rain erupted above them. Rand searched for a place to find cover, but like everyone else, they were stranded without shelter in an open field, surrounded by food trucks of every variety. Shelley laughed as a torrential, out of season monsoon rain drenched them.

Rand laughed with her, the heaviness of her feelings lifting as if rinsed away by the rain. She wrapped one arm around her waist, one behind her neck, and pulled her forward, their bodies connecting. Shelley gasped, laughter interrupted as Rand moved closer. Rand let go of Shelley's neck and moved to pull away, but Shelley responded, arms around Rand's neck. She slipped one into her hair and tried to stop her retreat. Rand was frozen, one hand still in the middle of Shelley's back.

Shelley whispered against Rand's ear, "Please." Rand didn't know what Shelley's plea was for, but she'd lost her ability to understand anything because all she knew was how Shelley's hands felt on her. "Rand, please."

Rand wrapped both arms around her waist and pulled her tight as the rain beat down. With Shelley in her arms, the grief and guilt Rand carried for years retreated from her consciousness. There was only Shelley. Then the rain stopped, and another thunderclap caused someone to bump into them and Rand let go as she stumbled. The sun broke through the clouds above. Shelley watched her, clothes drenched, face flushed.

Rand took her hand and pulled her forward. Shelley followed, and upon finding her way to Rand's side, grabbed her arm with her other hand. Rand pushed through the crowds and they stopped walking on the outer ring of the field. She faced Shelley.

"I don't know why I did that. I'm sorry if it wasn't welcome." Shelley placed both hands on Rand's shoulders. Rand had tears in her eyes, and Shelley looked at her with such compassion she felt like the sadness in her chest would spill out of her and flood the field. "I wanted to leave her." Shelley put her hands on Rand's shoulders, listening. "I was going to leave Kim. We'd been together since we were teenagers. I wasn't in love with her. I felt trapped. Then she got sick. This stuff with her parents. I feel like I deserve it."

"Did she know?"

"No, I mean, maybe. But she got sick before I could tell her. The day I was going to tell her. That's when she told me. When she found out about the cancer." Shelley dropped her hands and laced her fingers through Rand's, waiting. "I couldn't tell her."

"So you stayed with her, by her side?"

"Yes," Rand said. "She was so scared. I loved her. So much. I just wasn't in love with her and I wanted my freedom."

Shelley wrapped Rand in her arms, pulling her forward. Rand leaned stiffly into her arms and then relaxed, allowing herself comfort. Finally, Shelley spoke again.

"Rand, that's marriage." She pulled back so they could look at each other. "You know how many married couples aren't in love, would like their freedom, but stick it out, until death do they part, because they made a commitment? I mean, ideally, that comes with being in love, but often it doesn't. You still don't deserve this from her family. You don't."

Rand was suddenly aware of how cold and vulnerable she felt under drenched clothes. Sadness drained from her chest into her legs. They felt stapled to the earth, anchored and bolted down. Shelley pulled her forward this time. "Come on," Shelley said as they walked. "Let's order in and go back to my apartment. Dry off."

They walked silently through the parking lot. The dark storm clouds moved across the open expanse of desert sky, billowing black against the orange hue of sunset.

Shelley let go of Rand to get in the car. The warm air felt good after the chill of their wet clothes.

"I'm sorry for that," Rand said. She slipped the key into the ignition.

"For what?" Shelley paused, seat belt suspended midair.

"For all of it. I'm so emotional." Rand stared ahead. "I dropped a lot on you." Rand turned the key, and Shelley buckled her seat belt and then touched Rand's arm. Rand stared ahead.

"Look at me?" Shelley asked quietly. Rand steeled her nerve and faced her. "I'm going to come out. I'm going to tell the whole world I'm gay." Rand's face softened and she understood that Shelley was making herself vulnerable to her as well.

"Shelley," Rand said. "I, well, I'm happy for you. I don't even know what else to say." Shelley held her eyes and then looked away and shifted to sit back in her seat. Rand sat in the driver's seat and thought about Shelley in her arms just a few minutes prior, how she'd responded to her touch. "Shelley, have you ever, I mean, have you—"

"No," Shelley answered before she could finish. They sat silently for a few moments. Rand put the car in reverse and they left the food truck event.

"Rand, I really like you. The minute I saw you on that elevator. I'm ashamed to think that I offered to help you as a way to redeem myself. My father, it's just hard because I love him. It's so confusing. The organizations I've helped. In many ways, I feel so damaged. As much as all of that is true, I want to help you. Because I like you. Because you're genuinely one of the best people I know, and because I look forward to our conversations and the time we spend together like nothing else in my life."

"I guess we both feel guilty," Rand said. "When we both agree the other should not. You grew up in a constrictive environment, Shelley. It's natural it would take you time to understand yourself." Shelley turned up the radio and turned silently away from Rand. After a few minutes, Rand turned down the radio.

A few minutes passed. "I knew," Rand said.

"Knew what?"

"That you're gay," Rand said.

"Are you bragging?"

"Maybe," Rand said. "A little."

They drove to Shelley's apartment and walked silently up the stairs. Rand's clothes were mostly dry, but Shelley's hair was still wet so she excused herself to the bathroom. Rand heard her blow dryer turn on.

"Do you know what you want to order?" Rand called this out to Shelley, who returned to the room holding up a dry T-shirt for her. Rand slipped off her still slightly damp shirt, uncharacteristically bold, and slipped on the dry T-shirt. She looked up to see Shelley looking at her, the same unfixed gaze of desire on her face when she swept her into her arms at the park.

Rand thought about asking her again what food she wanted but couldn't find her words. Her gaze traveled down the length of Shelley's body, and she wondered how it might feel to sink into her, slip between her thighs, reach her fingers inside her warmth, feel her mouth open under hers. But she wouldn't do anything so dramatic. She forced her desire to retreat. What if she slept with Shelley and then decided she didn't want her? Shelley was so genuine and sensitive, and if Rand couldn't accept her completely, it would cause her considerable harm.

"We were going to order food," Rand said to break the silence.

"Let's do it," Shelley said.

CHAPTER EIGHTEEN

R and and Shelley sat at Jamie's kitchen table while she chopped tofu and vegetables for a stir-fry. Rachel tossed her phone on the table as she joined them.

"That was dramatic," Rand said.

"Thank you," Rachel said. "I also silenced it so no one can call me back to work. I need a break."

"Drama is underappreciated," Jamie said. Shelley laughed, enjoying the conversation. "Speaking of drama, I believe our government is falling apart."

"God, no politics," Rachel said. "No work phone and no politics."

"Why do you say that?" It was Shelley who spoke.

"See? She wants to talk about it," Jamie said, pointing at Shelley.

"It doesn't count. That's what she does for a living," Rachel said.

"It's true. She always wants to talk about politics," Rand said.

"Well, I like political and legal philosophy more than anything," Shelley said.

"I despise Trump," Jamie said. "How and why does your party continue to support him?"

"I can't speak on behalf of all Republicans," Shelley said. "I don't."

"Well, that's redemptive," Rachel said. "Sorry. I mean if you're Republican, at least don't like Trump."

"I think it's important to understand why he won," Shelley said. "His populist message struck a chord. And America's deep dislike for Hillary struck another."

"Populist message?" Jamie paused and turned to look at Shelley.

"He spoke to disenfranchised, working class whites who are frustrated with income stagnation and the growing wealth divide in America," Shelley said.

"You acknowledge an income divide," Jamie said. "If so, how can you support additional deregulation?"

"I'm not opposed to all regulation," Shelley said. "I'm likely more of a centrist than anything else. I like the free market. I like personal liberty and social mobility. There has to be a middle ground somewhere for all of us."

"Maybe you should register as an independent," Rachel said, breaking into the conversation.

"That's interesting," Shelley said. "Why do you say that?"

"Because you're too socially liberal to be a true Republican. But you're too fiscally conservative to be a Democrat."

"And you can't be gay and belong to a party that openly excludes you," Rand interjected.

"I tell you all the time that forty-four percent of Republicans support gay marriage, Rand. It's not all Republicans," Shelley said.

"It's all about the platform," Rand reiterated.

"Barry Goldwater, famous Arizona Senator, supported gay rights. Abortion rights. Believed the government's intrusion on these matters was wrong. Real western Libertarianism. Warned that Falwell was making the Republican party a religious organization," Shelley said.

"Ah, but he also opposed the Civil Rights Act," Jamie said. "I like to remind people of that when they try to hail him as a civil rights hero."

"He didn't oppose it conceptually. He always supported civil rights. He worried about overreach of the federal government with a few provisions of the final act," Shelley said, gently correcting Jamie. "It's not that those forty-four percent of Republicans don't believe in gay marriage rights or equal rights. It's not that we don't want people to have healthcare, living wages, and equal opportunity. We just don't believe the federal government is the best way to make all that happen," Shelley said.

"Let the market and free society do its thing?" Jamie turned back to food prep.

"Yes, and individuals, associating freely with one another," Shelley said.

"The only problem is that people won't do the right thing. If not for the Civil Rights Act, where would we be? It's necessary for the government to step in and stop abuses. Government can be a force for good, can be used to challenge socioeconomic, systemic oppression. Like these new bans on conversion therapy. It is absolutely necessary to protect LGBTQ+ youth from outdated, archaic, religious bullshit," Rand said.

"There might be a God," Shelley said.

"There is no God," Rand said.

"Oh my God," Rachel said. "Everyone shut up. Is the food ready?"

Jamie tossed the tofu in the skillet and held up her hand. "Five minutes," she said.

"Remember that guy with the sign in Manhattan?" Shelley put her hand on Rand's arm and felt her warm skin under her fingertips.

"I do," Rand said. "I almost forgot. What did the sign say?"

"The vortex is collapsing," Shelley said. "I think." She stared into Rand's eyes. Sometimes their conversations took a wrong turn and it made her uncomfortable. She was able to detach from ideas, view them conceptually, factually, without the emotion Rand attributed to them. It was likely because of their personality differences and Rand's life experience as an openly gay, gender nonconforming female. It was because of this that Shelley always wanted to be sure Rand was okay when they veered into potentially explosive territory.

"I understand your perspective," Shelley said to Rand. "I learn from it each time we talk."

"But," Rand said, waiting for more.

"Nothing," Shelley said, and Rand smiled at her.

"Sorry if I got strident," Rand said.

"Passionate," Shelley said. "And there may be a God."

Rachel laughed and nudged Shelley under the table with her foot. "Don't let her get away with anything, Shelley. Rand has believed she is right about everything since like, 1995."

"That is not true," Rand said.

"It is," Jamie said.

"I've noticed," Shelley agreed. "I mean, she's an activist for a reason." Rand waved her hands at Shelley and her friends, but laughed, calm restored. Shelley let go of her arm and tucked her hands under the table in her lap.

"Food is ready," Jamie said as she slid a bowl across the counter. Rachel brought it to the table and turned to take more from Jamie. Rand reached under the table and pulled Shelley's hand, threading their fingers together.

"Are you having fun?"

"Yes," Shelley said. "I am."

"I'm glad, but there is no God." Shelley laughed. Rand kissed her cheek and let go of her hand to take a bowl of salad from Rachel. She found Rand's defiance of God thrilling, and past the chasm of fear in her chest, it sparked something to life in her that day in the back of the cab. Rand's certainty gave her strength, even if she didn't always agree with her. Shelley hoped Rand drew as much from her but didn't think it was likely.

Rand seemed conflicted about their relationship. Today she was present, available, and engaged. A few days before when they met for lunch and a hike, Rand was distant, melancholy, and barely touched her. Shelley wanted more physical intimacy but knew, even with her limited experience, it was better not to push. Rand was worth waiting for, and it was possible that the resolution of the lawsuit would free her from the past so they could move forward together.

❖

Shelley stepped from Thirty Rock. A rainstorm stopped just a few minutes before. She'd waited in the dressing room and watched as the water cascaded down the sides of buildings, pounded awnings, and flooded the streets. Pedestrians scrambled under umbrellas and huddled together in clumps as they waited for lights to turn. From her perch above the noise, Shelley found it peaceful, even soothing. Though she knew the moment she stepped from the doors onto the street, the cold water would seep into her shoes, wind would sting her skin, and the rain would bounce from the umbrella with loud claps of sound.

So wisely, she waited. The storm had been torrential, but not long lasting, and the water already ran into sewers. Her flight to Phoenix was not leaving until the next morning. She'd talked with Rand, told her she was going to explore, and now longing for her swelled inside. She thought about Rand's presence next to her, and she wanted it all the time. She liked how it felt.

She wanted Rand.

But she still wasn't sure Rand wanted her.

Every new encounter with Rand awakened more feelings, and she was too in love to be terrified of them. Shelley wasn't young and had known enough mental illness to understand the truly transitory nature of life. Deep inside, Shelley felt some caution but chose again to ignore it. She was too engaged in the sensation of loving Rand that her normally conservative nature sublimated itself to her emotions.

She could only hope Rand felt the same, and that thought buoyed her through the worst moments of anxiety and uncertainty. It was a miracle, Shelley thought, to be in love.

She stood on the sidewalk, smiling up at the sky between buildings. A woman looked at her, in the disinterested way New Yorkers observe each other, half-aware of the other.

Shelley ducked her head down, momentarily embarrassed by her behavior, and pressed forward, wandering from block to block, the chilly, humid air a welcome respite from the scorching dry heat of the desert. Rand bought her a pair of AirPods, an unexpected gift before she left. When Shelley asked her why, Rand said, "It seems odd you have no headphones. I mean, who doesn't have headphones?"

Shelley slipped them from her pocket and put them in while she waited at a light on Eighth Avenue and Thirty-first Street. Madison Square Garden was in front of her, massive and forlorn, wet from the rain. She always thought the building looked sad. She opened Spotify on her phone, another new discovery via Rand, and chose a shared playlist. It was Rand's favorite songs, and Shelley didn't know all of the artists, but she was learning.

She wound down the busy streets around the square, crossed another intersection, turned a corner or two, not truly watching, just exploring, and then stopped, drawn forward by wrought iron gates and a courtyard. A statue of a saint stood in the middle, surrounded by the dark brick of the buildings on either side. New life sprouted on a bush, light green buds against the dead, oppressive concrete of the city.

Silence descended as Shelley stepped into the courtyard. The cacophony of Manhattan receded behind her. She walked toward the statue. St. Francis, flocked by animals, large and small. There was pressure in her chest, and momentarily, she feared a heart attack, remembering how her appendix had turned on her. But then, as the pressure mounted to a culminating peak, it dissipated, sending hot tendrils of energy through her arms and body. Shelley thought the absence of sound was evidence of her impending demise. She took three steps forward, looking for somewhere to sit. Rand's favorite music still played in her ears.

A family had commandeered the benches in the courtyard and so Shelley stumbled inside, into a beige hallway, down stairs, through other doors that opened into a chapel. There were rows of dark wood benches that matched the deep hue wood on the walls. She removed her headphones, and the silence swallowed her, and she stumbled to sit down on a bench toward the back.

The stained glass windows were beautiful. It was St. Francis, surrounded by animals, similar to the statue in the courtyard. She focused on the sheep, she didn't know why, and tried to count but was not able to do so. Her mind spun too quickly. Anxiety crept through her body like the coffee grounds she'd accidentally dumped across her kitchen floor the week before. She leaned heavily against the back of the bench and held her hands in her lap, putting her bag to the side of her. She interlaced her fingers, struggled to ground her emotions.

When she realized she was not going to be able to control the outcome of what was happening to her, she did something she'd never done before. She let go of her urge to try and rested her hands on either side of her body. A sob bent her over, and she covered her mouth. She cried silently in the back pew, tucked away from the world, and then the chorus began to sing. Vespers. Light filtered into the underground chapel, and a brilliant ray of light lit the middle of the church. She closed her eyes, wiped at her tears with the sleeve of her thermal, and set her glasses on her knee.

When she opened her eyes a few moments later, an older woman was sitting next to her. The woman smiled and took her hand. She wore her black hair close to her head, and her dark brown eyes twinkled with warmth and kindness. She patted Shelley's hand with one hand, held it with the other, and then released it.

"Crime to cry alone. Go on, then. Get it out," she said in a deep southern accent. Struck with the simple kindness of a stranger, Shelley continued to cry as the chorus filled the silence and the light moved through the chapel. When she was finished, as the chorus left, she became aware the woman next to her was gone, and she turned round and round to find her but wasn't able to do so.

Shelley's mystical experience rendered her helpless. Control was stripped away, her capitulation demanded. Shelley's despair grew stronger, overwhelming, and it was then that she felt the world was gone, and that only she remained. She imagined the universe, the vastness of it, and believed she stood alone in it. Everything around her slipped away, like a tablecloth in a magician's trick. The universe she was capable of seeing disappeared.

She was swept under, her will was nothing, and she didn't even fight. There was no resistance because there was nothing. Shelley was suspended somewhere, outside of time and space, where all is nothingness. The force was immense, the weight of it intense, burdening, and in it, she felt a moment of terror. She could not comprehend what had captured her, could not find the thoughts to understand what was happening. She was awed by a presence that overtook her, and it was an awe that made her tremor, shake, and feel weak.

Then, as suddenly as it came, the terror was replaced by an immense peace, a knowing, that the struggle means nothing, that life and death mean nothing. Her fear was stripped away, hesitation, doubt—all gone. All removed.

Shelley dwelled in knowing. There was no fear left—and because there was no fear, no despair. There was nowhere left to go. There was nothing to lose because nothing was ever lost. Life didn't end with death, but continued in different form, the universe infinite, and full of joy, love, and possibility.

Shelley settled, freed from her contact with the divine, and wiped her face. She climbed from the stairs with more awareness than she descended them. In the courtyard again, the normal sounds of the city returned, and she wondered where they went when she first entered the space. She stepped from the courtyard, onto the sidewalk, and the courtyard and church faded from view. She stopped to look behind her, but the iron fence around the courtyard didn't look as welcoming as it did when she first saw it. The space wasn't as illuminated as it first was.

The sky was brilliant blue above her. A taxi driver honked in the street. Someone yelled. Tourists laughed. A baby cried. She counted sixteen bricks below her feet. Shelley wanted to find a Starbucks, for coffee and a bathroom to rinse her face. A strange peace descended upon her, and inside, new thoughts organized themselves around understanding born during a visit with St. Francis in a Christian church. The irony of her encounter didn't escape her, but it felt like nothing her father offered. This felt like God should.

❖

Shelley sat on Tony's small sofa. They chatted as they watched the nightly news. She'd told him about her mystical experience in the midtown church and he teased her mercilessly.

"God loves gays," Tony said, enhancing the hints of a southern accent in his speech. His hair was perfectly styled, dark again, with bright orange highlights.

"I think God does," Shelley said with a grin and pushed his shoulder.

"Do you think there is a God?" Tony was suddenly serious. "Well, other than when you're yelling, 'God, Rand.'" Shelley laughed but ignored him. He continued. "Seriously, though."

"I mean, intelligent design is possible. A creator. I don't think God is who we grew up with, you know?"

"Not an old white guy, though, right?" Shelley agreed with him. "Don't vote Republican anymore. They're mean," Tony said.

"There are conservative principles I agree with," Shelley said.

"Money doesn't matter as much as kindness," Tony insisted.

"If we let go of our individual liberty to an authoritarian, parental state, who knows what we will end up with. We have to trust that state will always be governed by rational, just people, Tony, and history tells us that power can't be trusted to care about individuals." He waved his hand at her and fell silent. "The problem is an utter lack of regulation assigns that same power to corporations. We are incapable of nuanced political conversation." Shelley took a breath to continue, but Tony stopped her.

"God, Rand," he said. They laughed together and Shelley stood to use the restroom, checked her phone, and replied to a few comments on social media. She texted Rand that she missed her.

"Hurry up in there. It's time for the theater," Tony yelled.

She slipped on her shoes and followed him from the small apartment, enjoying herself but happy that she'd return home, to Rand, the next day.

CHAPTER NINETEEN

Rand's last patient for the day drained her. He refused to do anything significant to reorder his thinking or life but came every two weeks to complain about every aspect of it. The boss that criticized him constantly. The roommate who demanded rent money three days early. His mother who didn't like his tattoos or sexuality. Rand wanted to fire him as a patient and considered telling him she thought it best he move on. Refer him to another counselor. She finished her notes and slid them into his file, dropped them into the cabinet, and locked it with the key in her pocket.

The long walk out of the building was loud this time of night, the sound of footsteps reverberating in the empty space. The walls were hollow and the door to the stairwell clanged behind her. The late evening sun greeted her outside, the heat settling on her, seeping into her bones. Shelley was meeting her at her house. She'd not seen her since her return from Manhattan. Truthfully, Rand had avoided alone time with her.

Shelley filed the countersuit earlier in the day against Kim's parents. The process servers were delivering copies of the lawsuit to them as well. Rand thought this might be why she wanted to fire her client. There was only so much psychological space available in one person's head.

Shelley felt confident in the outcome of the lawsuit, which Rand read over the weekend while Shelley was out of town. Pages of claims, precedents, and outrage were on their way to them and their attorney. She slipped behind the driver's seat of her car. Sick dread filled her stomach and she rolled down the windows, letting the hot air escape. Rand rested her head on the steering wheel. Her phone rang, scaring her. It was Jamie.

"Yeah," she answered.

"Hi to you too. Whatcha doin'?"

"Feeling nauseous in my car outside the office," Rand answered, turning on the ignition.

"'K, maybe start the car and drive home. Rachel and I talked to Shelley. We are ordering dinner, to hang tonight." Rand sighed and Jamie continued. "Don't sigh. People love you whether you like it or not."

"I'm just overwhelmed."

"You're always overwhelmed. Time to let go. Live a bit. Be where you are. You have a hot new conservative girlfriend."

"Stop. She's not my girlfriend. Or that conservative." Was she either?

"Are you serious? She's mad for you. Did you read her article about abortion? Whatever. She has pretty hair. Come on. Stop being so emo and come home."

Rand hung up the phone and backed up. She'd not actually read any of Shelley's most recent work. She'd missed her last appearance on MSNBC and had not followed up to watch it as she should have. Shelley was completely invested in her, but she felt tied to Kim, even though the tendrils of the past were lessening around her heart. Was that the reason? Was she still tied to Kim? Sometimes, she saw Shelley and wanted her. Getting involved with Shelley as she had might not have been the best course of action. At least she'd not slept with her yet.

Mary refused to offer judgment, though she openly expressed concern about their different world views. Surprisingly, Rand had not thought much about that, but then, the topic had never presented itself in such a way that she felt they should discuss it. Even when Shelley brought it up, as though she were concerned, Rand had not been. Despite her urge to flee, when she looked at the time they'd spent together, she acknowledged she felt comfortable with Shelley, and maybe that worried her as well.

She was comfortable with Kim and didn't want to fall into the same trap. She also didn't want to take advantage of Shelley, who was obviously in love with her. Rand wasn't sure she reciprocated, but didn't feel fully available, either, so her emotions felt suspect, even to herself. But Shelley adored her. Rand could see it in every glance, word, and moment they spent together. They'd spent hours together and it was nothing like her relationship with Kim. Rand felt like she was spinning in circles around her feelings like a fidget-spinner.

Being so desired was a new experience for Rand and likely contributed to some of her overwhelming feelings. She was surprised they moved into such emotional intimacy so quickly, but they'd corresponded for almost a year. Jamie told her not to overthink it, but she worried about how much she was risking versus Shelley, and when she told Jamie this her response was, "Well, then risk the same!"

Also, Rand thought with a sneer at her phone, she was not emo. Jamie had room to talk, given how madly in love she was with her best friend, though she'd never admit it, and with that thought, she dialed Rachel, who answered quickly.

"Rachel," Rand said.

Rachel answered. "Rand. You never call. Are you okay?"

"I am. Are you at my house yet?"

"No. Just out of the shower. On my way soon."

"Hey, how conservative is Shelley?"

"Does it matter, Rand?" Rand didn't answer. "You knew who she was when you met her. She might have escaped Evangelicalism, but…" Rachel trailed off.

"Conservatism isn't evil," Rand said, thinking out loud.

"No, it's not. I have conservative edges about some issues. Personal responsibility. Social mobility. Taxes."

"Right," Rand agreed. "It's just that I suddenly feel really worried about it. Like, if I had a kid and they came home and told me they'd become a Christian Republican, well, I'd likely want to disown them. That's pretty awful, right?"

"I mean, I get it. Like some Christians with gay or transgender kids," Rachel said.

"She didn't vote for Trump, remember," Rand said.

"Are you looking for reasons to not be with her?"

Rand turned down the street to her house. "I'm almost home."

"Think about it," Rachel said. "I think you're trying to find stuff to be wrong. See you soon."

Rand pulled into the garage, which was already open, waiting for her. Shelley's modest sedan was parked on the road and Jamie's moped, with the traveling basket for the beagles, was inside the courtyard. Rachel hated the moped and often texted Jamie pictures of mangled bodies after motorcycle accidents. Jamie countered she lived in the same development as Rand, a few blocks away, so it was like riding a bike.

Shelley and Jamie waited in the front room, and the beagles greeted her with excitement. Shelley met her eyes and smiled so sincerely Rand felt momentary discomfort for her conversation with Rachel. Rand sat next to Shelley on the couch. Shelley looked at her with so much affection and warmth that squirming felt like the only alternative. Kim hadn't looked at her like that. She might have felt comfortable with Kim, but she'd never felt so desired. She had no other experience, and for a moment, her flight responses were triggered, and running out the back door of her own house seemed like the best course of action.

The doorbell rang and Shelley stood up. "That's the food."

Shelley touched Rand's shoulder as she walked by her, and Jamie mouthed, "What is wrong with you?" Rand ignored her and stood to go to the door with Shelley. She took the bags from her hand as Shelley signed the receipt. Both beagles now sat on Jamie's lap. When Rand turned to look at Jamie, she mouthed, "Emo" to her and Rand mouthed back, "F off."

❖

Later, after dinner, they sat on the back patio. Rand started the propane fire pit, even though it was warm, and Jamie turned on the misters. Rachel said, "This is ridiculous. We have a fire going, with misters, and it's ninety-five degrees out here."

"Should I turn off the fire?" Rand turned the knobs and cut off the propane.

"Nah," Rachel conceded. "I kind of liked it. I just felt the need to say it. Though it's too late now." Shelley laughed and sipped her wine. Rachel watched Rand, who stared at the fire pit, reserved and quiet. She nudged Jamie with her foot and stood. "We'll clear out of here." Jamie whistled to the dogs.

"You don't need to go," Rand said.

"I work a long shift tomorrow at noon. Would like to get some sleep."

Jamie clipped the leashes on the beagles. "Yeah, me too."

Rachel raised an eyebrow, but Rand spoke. "If only all of us could have your schedule." She handed Rachel the dogs' leashes and they left together, negotiating her use of the moped after dark. The door to the garage sounded behind them and Shelley sat forward, setting her glass on the fire pit.

"What's wrong?" Shelley sat on the bench next to Rand, hands on her arm. Rand looked at Shelley's hands and felt their warmth. Thought about kissing her, resting in her arms. They could go inside, up the stairs and crawl into bed. Thought about the scathing lawsuit Shelley drafted on her behalf. Shelley had never held anything back from her, and when she looked up to meet her eyes, it was clear she still wasn't. So why were her politics suddenly an issue? Was it connected to the lawsuit? An avenue for guilt? Guilty energy needed release and a target.

"I'm just tired, I think."

"Okay," Shelley said. "I'll let you rest and be." She stood and picked up her glass. Rand watched her walk into the house, saw her silhouette in the window by the sink, heard the water turn on. She should follow her, she thought. Chase her down, tell her not to leave. That was the right thing to do. But Rand felt paralyzed. Something in the middle of her was frozen. The fire of grief and guilt was replaced with an iceberg. Somewhere on it, a polar bear was starving. Shelley came to the sliding glass door, purse on her shoulder.

"I'm going to head home." Rand was still frozen. "I wish you'd let me in," Shelley said.

"I do," Rand said.

"No, you don't. I assume it's the lawsuit. Or maybe you just don't feel the same. I'll give you space." Rand thought about this, closed her eyes, and when she opened them, Shelley was gone, and she wanted to follow but could not.

❖

Rand sat in Mary's office, legs under her like she was in kindergarten. Mary commented on it. "You are sitting like you've regressed."

"I've been doing yoga," Rand snapped.

"You're angry," Mary said

"Maybe." Mary raised her eyebrow and put the notebook down. She stared at Rand.

"You're angry because I questioned your relationship with Shelley last time."

"Maybe." Rand pulled her legs from underneath her and stretched them out in front of her. She put her hands on the floor. "I'm frozen. Like you hear stories about people who get lockjaw. Only, I have lockgut, or something." She sat up and put her hand on her stomach. "Right here. It's like the arctic in there."

"What happened?"

"Shelley drafted and filed a lawsuit against Kim's parents and their attorney. For harassment. Readied a complaint with the state bar if he doesn't back down. It was scathing. So angry." Mary said nothing. Rand looked at the clock above her head. The battery needed to be replaced because it said two fifteen p.m. every time she came to the office and it was eleven thirty in the morning. She pointed at it. "You need a new battery." Mary watched her.

"Shelley is brilliant. She can write like a dream. We've been emailing for almost a year, you know? When she traveled, she sent me emails in the morning and I'd read them again and again."

"Maybe it isn't rash. Maybe it's love."

"I'm frozen. You were right. I shouldn't have become involved with her. I'm letting her fix my issues with Kim's parents. That's not healthy, right?"

"Why let her help and no one else?" Rand shrugged. "That was my point last time, had you held still and let me finish. So many people have offered to help you. You have resources and means. So why Shelley? Why did you say yes to her?"

Rand sat back on the couch and put her hands in her hair. "Jamie says I'm emo." Mary laughed. "Don't laugh."

"You're really emotional. It's okay."

"I know. Totally emo is what she said." Mary laughed again and now Rand did as well.

"Why did you let her help you?"

Rand held eye contact with Mary. "I feel safe with her." Mary stared at her. Rand knew she was checking for inconsistency between her words and movements. "I got so mad at you because you were right and also, because you were wrong. I feel safe with her. She's in love with me and looks at me like no one ever has before. She's pretty and a vegan.

Also, a Republican. It's weird. I just know I feel safe. I've not pushed for anything more."

"And you desire her?"

"God, yes," Rand said.

"You have different world views, values."

"I think you're projecting," Rand said.

"Likely, but it's still true. I mean, Rand, for Christ's sake, she's a Republican."

"She is," Rand said. "Do you think I should probably talk to her about it? It's not like I've just learned she's a serial killer and have to decide whether to stay or not. I mean, she's just a Republican."

"I'm more your friend right now than your therapist, and I have such strong political opinions from years of treating patients from conservative families. It's not about taxes or regulation. It's about energy. Watch the Republican National Convention and they all wear suits and look like businessmen in boardrooms. It's a sea of cis gendered, heteronormative, white people. Watch a Democratic National Convention and people are free, different, and exactly who they are."

"I get it," Rand said. "Shelley fits in at the RNC. She always wears these super conservative clothes. Pulls her hair up. Holds herself just so. Measures every word. I kind of like it." Mary shook her head. "What? I do."

"I'm just telling you that it's likely to become an issue at some point. Our times are so polarized. I'll let it be in case I'm projecting."

"Noted," Rand said.

"Let's talk about why you're frozen." Rand sighed and looked back at the clock. It still said two fifteen p.m.

"Kim."

"Kim's been dead for years now, Rand. What are you really hanging on to at this point? And why? Do you want to be unhappy? You've formed an attachment, I think, to your own guilt. You use that to derail any possible happiness."

"Ouch," Rand said, turning away from Mary.

"Do you agree?"

"What if I am just using Shelley?" Rand said.

"Are you using Shelley?"

"Stop asking me questions and answer me. Help me."

Mary sighed, pushed her bobbed hair behind her ears, took off her glasses, and set them behind her on the desk. "Rand," she said. "Stop it."

"I'm sorry."

Mary acknowledged her with a wave. "Are you using Shelley?"

Rand bent over again. "I don't think so. I genuinely enjoy her company. I find comfort in her. I think she enjoys being with me."

"Okay, so let go of that. I think you're projecting guilt from Kim toward Shelley." Rand looked at the time on her watch.

"I've kept you long enough." Rand stood. Mary slumped down in her chair and shook her head. "Did I break you?"

"Maybe," Mary said. "I liked it better when we were just friends."

"Yeah," Rand said. "Well, tell that to Jamie. She'd disagree."

CHAPTER TWENTY

Rand returned to her office, met with two patients, saw them out, and now sat behind her desk, laptop open. She searched for Shelley's name and clicked on the first image of her. It took her to a gallery of pictures from over the years. Shelley standing with her family in the late 1990s. Shelley with her father in the early 2000s, next to George W. Bush. A picture of Shelley just three years before, consulting with the Republican Governor's Association for Obamacare.

Each click took Rand deeper into Shelley's public life. She read briefs filed by her, in the same clear language she'd used to write the suit for Rand. She saw the picture snapped of Shelley in the Manhattan bar. She found an article about abortion, where Shelley argued the only way to stop abortion was education, contraceptive access, and social support like healthcare and education to work programs for the mother unable to afford it on her own.

Shelley wrote, "I think life should protect life. It's why I don't eat animals. I don't like abortion. Sit with the idea of a human life, growing in its most vulnerable moments, dying at our hand. It's an atrocious thought. I'm conflicted, of course, because ever more atrocious is the idea of an unwanted child born, suffering in poverty, abused, or neglected. I don't think the answer to this is to kill the child as fetus, but to either prevent the fetus's existence to begin, or to address critical social issues that create adverse scenarios once the child is born. All of these solutions are nuanced and require more than a Tweet or tagline, accusation or partisanship. Taking each idea, one at a time, let's start with prevention. Republicans must concede and provide public access to sex education, contraception, and women's healthcare. Because study after study shows the best way to stop unwanted pregnancy is to educate women…"

The article continued, and Rand read every word it, almost fatigued as she came to the end. It was posted just a few weeks earlier. It received a fair amount of media coverage, was quoted and cited in the *Washington Post* and the *New York Times*. It was the article Jamie mentioned. Shelley's argument was logical and coherent. Brilliant. If she were wise, she'd fall madly in love with her. Why couldn't she?

She spent hours this way, reading archived articles about Shelley's dad and his dad before him. She read every page on his website, cringing when she read the articles about faith-based marriage and the sin of homosexuality. She'd known who Shelley was when they met in that elevator, in what felt like another life, but she'd not confronted it with such visceral understanding before.

Finally, exhausted by her search, she closed her laptop and looked out the window. The sun had almost disappeared, and the sky around it was tinged with bright red and orange. She left the office and drove home to meet Shelley, who arrived just as she finished a glass of wine.

They drove together to meet with Kim's parents and their attorney. Rand said very little, once again wishing she'd never involved Shelley in this endeavor. Shelley parked the car in the open parking lot of the small law firm office off Seventh Avenue and Thomas. Rand was frozen, her breath tight in her chest. She stared straight ahead. Shelley reached a tentative hand across the middle console and touched Rand's arm. Rand met her gaze, eyes wide and unfixed.

"Come on," Shelley said, opening the car door. "Let's get this over with." Rand followed her, quietly, and suddenly, took her hand, needed to feel her close. A wave of nausea overtook Rand and she felt as though she were slipping through the cracks of the sidewalk as they walked. Just under the shade of the entrance door opening, Shelley stopped walking and put her hands on Rand's shoulder, squaring them face-to-face.

"Don't talk," Shelley said. "I will do all the talking, okay? Agree to nothing. Say nothing," she emphasized, and Rand nodded. "Let me handle this okay? Understand?" Again, Rand agreed relinquishing control in a way she'd never known possible. They walked through the sliding doors together, were greeted with a great blast of cold air, and Rand took a deep breath, finding her calm and center. The lobby was modest, with polished beige tile and new, stiff, brown furniture. A receptionist sat behind the small desk and greeted them with a smile.

"We're here to meet with David Smith," Shelley said. Rand looked at her. She hadn't even known the attorney's name. Rand stood behind Shelley as if she were hiding and chided herself. She was a grown adult and had regressed to a disturbing degree. She stepped up to the side of Shelley, asserting her equal status.

They sat on the couch in the lobby. The fabric was rough and stiff. "It itches," Shelley said and stood up but kept her hand on Rand's shoulder, insisting it was fine for her to sit. They waited like that, Rand on the couch, in dark jeans and a button-down, while Shelley stood next to her in a dark suit with heels, hair pulled back in a tight bun. Rand saw their reflection in the mirror. Yin and yang, she thought, looking from her own reflection to the real life Shelley, standing with impeccable composure.

The door opened and a man in a suit approached them, hand out to Shelley. "David Smith," he said. Shelley took his hand, shook it firmly, introduced herself, and then put her hand back on Rand's shoulder, as if to reassure her. "We're ready in the meeting room."

Rand stood and David reached out his hand to her, but she didn't take it. He dropped his hand and walked ahead of them. Rand and Shelley followed him down the long hallway, and turned into a conference room. Kim's parents, Jack and Donna, were already there and sat across the table. The thought ricocheted around her head like a pellet in a pinball machine. She'd not seen them since Kim's funeral, and before then it had been years. Kim finally absolved herself of responsibility for them and declared she would never speak to her family again a decade before she died.

Rand sat across from them and made eye contact, her earlier panic and fear replaced with anger and indignation. Suddenly, she remembered them as they were when she and

Kim were teenagers. They lived through their children's achievements, sucking the lifeblood from them, vampire parents. Her mother was a narcissist, and now, on this side of everything that happened, Rand realized she was controlling. With these memories flooding her, Rand realized that they were not homophobic. This wasn't about their marriage, or their daughter's sexuality. They were angry that Kim got away and then died and they blamed Rand for it.

"We received your lawsuit," David said, beginning the conversation.

"Good," Shelley said, opening a folder, voice dispassionate.

"We think it's without merit," David added.

"Maybe," Shelley said, "but I'm willing to find out what a judge thinks." She looked up, made eye contact with each one of them.

"My clients simply want your client to give them access to their dead daughter's things so they can reclaim their priceless family heirlooms."

"She's done that," Shelley said. Her tone was still so dispassionate, Rand looked at her with a sense of awe. Flat and chilled, like she took her voice box out and stuck it in the freezer for a while. It was also really sexy. Rand was confused by a bombardment of emotions, all at once.

"They believe she is withholding a broach, emerald ring, and a diamond necklace. My client's daughter took these things without authorization and they want them back. In total, they are worth sixty thousand dollars." David pushed pictures across the table with an estimate sheet from a jeweler.

"My client has already been through this with you. She doesn't have these items in her possession. This same issue, or variations of it, comes up again and again." Shelley sat back, not touching the pictures.

"Where are they?" Kim's mother shouted. "I know you're lying!"

"How many times does she need to tell you?" Shelley spoke directly to Kim's mother, tone firm but not unkind.

"As many times as we need to get to resolution," David said.

"You think a judge can make things materialize out of thin air?" David stared at her. "Because you know there is nothing to be done legally, but you're hoping that continued pressure will change Rand's mind? Somehow make her conjure these items and return them?"

David sat back, arms folded over his chest. Shelley continued.

"Here is where we are. Rand has no idea where these items are. None. They are not in her possession. She remembers Kim selling some things in their early twenties to pay her tuition, when they refused." Shelley pointed at Kim's parents. "But none of this is Rand's drama. This belongs to your clients and their daughter." Donna and Jack gasped. "At this point, your lawsuit is just one final step into full-blown harassment. This first lawsuit for damages is just my start. I will bury you in civil tort cases for the rest of your lives if you keep this up."

Rand looked at Shelley. She was scathing and terrifying. How could she be as sensitive and thoughtful as she was, and as terrifying? David felt it. Rand watched his body movements stiffen.

"You," Shelley said, pointing at David, "I will report to the Bar. I'll file a complaint asking the court to label you as vexatious litigants and you a vexatious litigator." Shelley took another file from her folder and slid it across the table. "Just so you're clear. That's lawsuit number two, suing your clients for emotional distress and legal fees. I'm asking for two hundred fifty thousand. I've not filed it yet, but I will. I'll give you seventy-two hours to decide."

David looked at his clients, who stared at Shelley with barely contained rage. Donna hit the table and Jack stood up, the chair crashing behind them into the wall. Shelley reached and put her hand on Rand's arm when she started and moved to flee.

"It's okay," Shelley said quietly to Rand.

Shelley then turned to David. "Your clients need good advice, David, and what you're doing right now isn't serving them. It's time everyone moved on."

He didn't respond immediately. "You're posturing. Bluffing."

"I suppose we will see. Are you sure you want to deal with it?" Shelley held eye contact with him, a steely reserve Rand had never seen before. Shelley's energy was hardened, her gaze strong, her body unmoving. The amount of emotional work Shelley had done to arrive to that kind of steely resolve, as sensitive as she was, was incredible. It also explained why she stopped practicing law daily and decided to write.

"We'll be in touch with our decision." David broke eye contact first. Shelley won the standoff.

Shelley moved her hand under Rand's arm, urged her to stand. She left it there, gripping her forearm, her thumb rubbing a reassuring pattern on her skin. "I'll leave that draft lawsuit here for you to consider with your decision. I'd rather not file it." Rand turned to leave with her and stopped at the door, turning to look at Donna and Jack.

"I'm so sorry for your loss," Rand said, struck with a sudden desire for closure. "I miss her too." Donna turned away from her, but Jack held eye contact and watched as she left the room.

CHAPTER TWENTY-ONE

Rand climbed into the front seat of Shelley's car, put her chin in her hand, and stared out the window. Shelley started the car and put on her sunglasses. She sat with her hands in her lap and then adjusted the air vents.

"Are you okay?" Rand was silent, still staring out the window. "Rand?" Shelley implored, tone desperate. "Please respond."

"I shouldn't be so shaken," Rand said.

"Lawsuits are stressful. It's a lot of heavy energy," Shelley said. "I don't think I realized how heavy until today. Sitting in that room, I felt like I was under a mudslide."

Rand turned toward her, suddenly less preoccupied with herself. "Are you okay?"

"Oh yes, I'm fine," Shelley said as she reached for Rand's hand. "I think I'm so emotionally involved with you, your energy, that the weight of the whole situation is bleeding into my space."

"I shouldn't have asked you to help me with this."

"Once again, I offered." Shelley put the car in reverse. Rand looked at her, felt her calm strength, and realized how much more confident she seemed since they met in Manhattan. "We can't undo my helping now. Let's just figure out a way forward. Let's see if this helps you move forward."

"Want to come over?" It was Rand's tentative reach through the dense energy between them.

Shelley didn't respond immediately and then said, "I think maybe I'll go home. I have some work to do."

Dread erupted in Rand's chest. She breathed through the fear but got stuck on the edges of it. It was likely best they separate for a bit. Amidst all her worry about herself, she hadn't considered it might be difficult for Shelley to face her wife's parents. Even if she didn't articulate it, that had to be uncomfortable. Rand didn't consider herself selfish, but she'd been so with Shelley.

"Shelley," she spoke. "Had Kim not died, I would have divorced her. And likely, we'd still have met and we'd be where we are." Shelley's jaw tightened. They stopped at a stop light and Rand watched a homeless person drag a shopping cart across the street, loaded with black plastic bags and blankets. Rand watched Shelley's gaze follow the person, her breath a bit heavier than she'd seen it before.

"It's tough to take comfort in the idea that someone died."

"I didn't mean it like that. I was just thinking it was so selfish of me to allow you to do this, that it might have been painful for you." Rand looked out the window, following the shopping cart as its owner wound around the back of the Circle K. The light changed and Shelley pulled through the light. The summer sun began its descent but still shone so brightly white-hot rays bounced from the hood of the car.

Shelley turned into Rand's housing development. The stark asphalt of the urban sprawl gave way to well-tended sidewalks with tile and designs.

"Rand," she said, softly, slowly. "I'm a free individual, completely autonomous, and while in the process of discovering myself, more than capable of tending to my own emotional needs."

"Wow," Rand said angrily.

"What?" Shelley asked, indignation rising.

"I didn't suggest you were not any of those things," Rand said. Her skin felt blistered, though she knew it wasn't.

"You may as well have. You're so wrapped up in your own self-created drama."

"Oh, I am?" Rand pointed at her chest. "My drama is not real? It doesn't meet your exacting standards? Says the woman who isn't even out. Who supports a political party who denigrates her personally."

Shelley stopped in front of Rand's house. "I'll let you out here."

Rand sighed. "Shelley, I don't know why I said that. I'm sorry. That was cruel."

"It's fine. Just get out. We can talk tomorrow."

Rand reached across the console and touched her arm, and Shelley looked up and met her eyes. "I'm sorry."

"Yes," Shelley said, her voice softened, "Me too."

Rand wanted to kiss her, but there was nothing in Shelley's body language that said it was welcome. Rand grabbed the door handle, pushed it open, and stepped from the car. She shut the door and watched Shelley pull away. She meandered slowly into her front courtyard, stopping to fill the fountain.

Heat was heavy on her back and her shirt stuck to her with sweat. She took it off and threw it at the front door. She wore a tight underwear tank top, and the sun on the bare skin of her arms felt almost painful. Rand bent and picked up her shirt, opened the front door with her key, and stripped off the rest of her clothes as she walked through the house.

She opened the sliding glass door and tread across the lawn. Rand jumped into the pool. Floating on her back, the heavy sun on her skin, she closed her eyes, dreadfully tired of herself. She wasn't ready to be involved with someone, and it had been rash, if not desperate, to become so emotionally involved with Shelley. She'd misused her obvious attraction for her because Rand was lonely.

But if that was the case, why did the idea of not talking with her make her feel nauseous? Rand climbed from the pool and walked into the house, grabbed a bottle of wine, and returned. She stepped in, sitting on the steps, naked, drinking wine directly from the bottle. Rand considered calling Jamie but then changed her mind. She scooted down farther into the pool and sat on the bottom stair.

Her phone was somewhere in the house and she didn't care. She took another long swig of the wine, and then set it on the edge of the pool and then sunk under the water. She swam to the middle of the pool. The water rippled around her. Then, thunder cracked and a few moments later, lightning burst across the darkening sky, followed by more rumbling thunder. Rand reluctantly swam to the side of the pool, grabbed her wine bottle, and climbed out.

As she walked, the monsoon rain began, warm against her naked body. She sat on the bench and crossed her legs, wine bottle in one hand. Inside, her phone rang but she ignored it. Then, her garage door opened but she didn't care about that either. A few moments later, the sliding glass door opened, and she jumped.

Jamie yelled, then covered her eyes with both hands. "I'm going to die. I'm never going to be the same."

"You've seen me naked before," Rand said, sitting back down, crossing her legs again, with the wine bottle tipped back. It was empty. She shook it, trying to get more out.

"Jesus," Jamie said as she stepped into the house. "I'll get you more." She came back out a few moments later with an opened bottle and held a glass for herself. Rand took the bottle and drank from it. Jamie sat next to her.

"Should I take off my clothes too?"

"If you want." Rand shrugged. The wind picked up and a pot blew over.

"I'm suggesting, just suggesting," Jamie said, "that we go inside. Given a monsoon is coming, things start getting blown over, and you might get injured in any of your tender wenders." She pointed at Rand, moving her finger up and down as if to map her body.

Rand sighed, took another swig, and shrugged.

"Up," Jamie said. "Inside." Rand complied. Jamie walked in front of her into the house, disappearing down the hall to get her robe. She tossed it to Rand. "Please put that on." Jamie sunk into a chair across from her.

Rand put one arm in the robe and draped the rest of it over her, cold from the air conditioning. She looked at Jamie, felt the effects of the wine, and tipped the bottle toward her before taking another drink.

"I take it the meeting with the attorney went well?"

"Shelley was fierce. They'll drop it now. I'm sure."

"Where is Shelley?" Jamie asked.

"Mad at me," Rand said.

"Why?"

"I was overly patronizing, probably. I accused her of not having any moral high ground about anything because she isn't out and is a Republican."

"Ouch," Jamie said, sipping her wine. She watched Rand, a look of alarm on her face, and quietly slipped her phone from her pocket.

"Are you telling Rachel on me?"

"Yes," Jamie answered as she texted. "I'm telling her it may be necessary to check you in somewhere."

"I can get drunk and swim naked," Rand snapped. "It's allowed." She held up her hands, one holding the bottle. Then she dropped her arms and drank more.

"Okay," Jamie said. "That's enough. Give me the wine." She walked to her, reached for the bottle, and Rand yanked it away.

"I'm fine. I am a therapist, you know. I'm in touch with my feelings. And right now, I think I am just relieving stress. Like a pressure gauge, you know? It was a big day."

"And then you alienated a woman who's made you happier than you've ever been in your life and sent her away after she fixed it for you?" Jamie succeeded in grabbing the bottle. "What are you doing?"

Rand looked at Jamie, lurched forward for the bottle, but then accepted defeat. She collapsed back onto the couch, wrestling to get her other arm in the robe. It was on backward, but she didn't care.

"I am so sick of myself," Rand said, words slurred. She'd not eaten dinner and the wine settled heavy in her limbs. Her stomach turned. She jumped from the couch and rushed into the bathroom, throwing up just as she hit the toilet.

"Fuck me," Jamie said as she came in a few moments later with a cold washcloth. "Dude, I'm having flashbacks of life at twenty-one." Rand flushed the toilet and took the washcloth and wiped her face.

"Oh my God. Why did I drink two bottles of wine?

"Technically, it was a bottle and about three-quarters. I had some and took it away before you finished." Jamie leaned against the sink.

The robe still on backward, Rand slumped against the bathtub, then climbed up and dropped into it. The cold felt good against her back.

"I'm just going to be here for a while," Rand said.

Jamie flushed the toilet again, walked from the room, and returned with a glass of water. Rand took it and sipped. Jamie sat next to her on the floor, her back against the wall, feet between the toilet and tub.

Rand sipped more water, some semblance of calm returning to her. "Should I eat?"

"Um, probably not right now. Maybe in a bit," Jamie said. Rand agreed and drank more water. "Are you going to break up with her?"

"Technically, we're not dating. We just email five times a day, text all the time, and spend all our free time together," Rand said, angry.

"Dude," Jamie said.

Rand sat quietly, staring at the faucet. A tiny droplet of water formed. She moved to stick her toe to stop it and the skin on her back and ass squeaked.

"You dealt it," Jamie said and they both laughed.

"I'm more of a mess than I thought," Rand said. Jamie was quiet. "You didn't disagree."

Jamie was holding her phone, scrolling through Spotify. She pulled up their shared playlist of favorite songs. The Indigo Girls, and Jewel filled the silent space of the bathroom. Rand said, "Lilith Fair revisited." Jamie laughed but they fell silent again, listening to another song. "How did we get here?" Rand had lost so much time. So many years between those songs and the moment she was in. Kim was dead. She had wanted to divorce her. She was forty.

"To the bathroom? You puked up two bottles of red wine," Jamie said.

"You said a bottle and three-quarters," Rand said. Jamie grinned. "I mean, here. To forty. Me with a dead wife. You sitting next to me because I'm having a bad day and my new girlfriend is a Republican. How did we get to midlife?"

Jamie stood and helped Rand out of the tub. Rand put her arms around Jamie's neck. "We're going to die one day."

"We all do," Jamie said.

"Days turn into years. Our lives just slip by us. Our dreams. What we thought it would look like. None of it matters. I'm not sure it does."

"Okay, Camus, let's get you to bed," Jamie said.

Rand let Jamie lead her into her bedroom. "What matters, Jamie?" Rand slipped out of the robe and climbed between the sheets.

"This," Jamie said, sitting by her on the bed. "Friendship. Love. Coffee. Beagles."

"I can't feel anything," Rand said.

"I know," Jamie said, hand on Rand's head. "You will. It's just part of the process. You're letting go. I think there is always this kind of nothingness in the midst of loss. Destruction. You'll wake up, one day soon, on the other side of this. Know how I know?"

"No," Rand said.

"Because that's what you told me, about ten years ago. Remember? When I was so depressed." Rand closed her eyes and tried to attach to an observer's perspective about her own behavior but could not. The room began to spin so she shifted and put her foot on the floor next to Jamie, who moved, climbing over her to sit next to her on the bed. She turned on the television.

"I'll stay a while. Sleep," Jamie said as Rand settled into wine's deep sleep, one foot still on the floor.

CHAPTER TWENTY-TWO

Rand had eleven text messages—from Jamie, Rachel, her mom, and just one from Shelley. She read that one first. Shelley wanted to know how she was, in her simple direct language. She was the only person Rand knew who used complete sentences with punctuation in text. Rand replied and asked her for dinner. Shelley responded immediately, as she always did. Rand opened her desk drawer and took aspirin. Her late night adventures with wine weighed heavily on her.

Rand replied quickly to everyone else, gathered her things, and left the building. The temperature had dropped about seven degrees, a result of the monsoon the night before, and she appreciated it. Shelley was to meet her at the restaurant, and though unsure what she was going to say, Rand knew it needed to be done.

The drive was quick. Rand was not surprised to see Shelley's car in the parking lot of the small Indian restaurant where they'd agreed to meet. Shelley was always punctual, always did what she agreed to do. Shelley smiled when she saw Rand and stood to hug her as she came to the table. It was just twenty-four hours since their weird argument after the attorney's office, though it seemed like much longer. Rand hugged Shelley back, a kind of desperation rising inside, as she was overcome with a desire to just go home and rest in her arms. Rand let go.

"Are you okay?" Shelley's tone was soft, tentative.

Shelley's hair was pulled back in a tight bun. She wore dark slacks and a blouse, and shoes with a small heel. Rand thought about Mary and agreed that Shelley's energy was different from most of her friends. Why was that though? Culture? Nurturing? How could anyone queer grow up in such an environment and thrive anyway? Shelley was living testament to the capacity of unique human identity to persevere against oppressive social norms. Even though everything about Shelley indicated order, control, and reason. She found her own unique identity, but it was not the free expression Rand grew up with and knew with Jamie and Rachel and her other friends.

But Rand knew she wasn't cold, even if she struggled to express emotion. She was capable of deep affection and loyalty as well. Shelley's posture was perfect, back straight, elbows off the table. She held her body with so much conscious intention, Rand wondered what she would look like if she let herself be and rest.

Shelley was also intuitive, and Rand saw dread rise in her. Rand reached out her hand instinctively. Shelley kept her hands in her lap and asked, "Are you breaking up with me? I mean if we are even dating to break up? You're so confusing, Rand."

Rand looked down at the table. There were tears in Shelley's eyes she didn't want to see. "Did you use me to write that suit?"

"God, no," Rand said. "I wish I'd never agreed to let you help me. It was inappropriate. I shouldn't have involved you."

Shelley took off her glasses, covered her eyes for a moment, and set her glasses on the table. "I offered. It doesn't matter. I heard from the attorney today. He's filing to drop the suit. He's also informed his clients he won't do any additional work for them and has advised them to stop their legal pursuit of you. It's done anyway. Over. If they come back, you have this precedent now and another attorney can help you."

Rand looked at her, confused, overwhelmed, and grateful. "Shelley, I—" Rand struggled for words and looked at the painting on the wall behind Shelley's shoulder. The server arrived with their food, setting it between them on the table, oblivious to their awkward silence.

Shelley spoke first, when the server left. "I ordered our food. Your favorite. The eggplant." Then tears escaped her eyes and she wiped them quickly with her fist. "Why?" Shelley met Rand's eyes.

"We're from two completely different worlds, first. I worry it will be an issue at some point. Also, Shelley, I just barely read your articles from the last month. I didn't even watch you on television last week. I think you probably deserve that kind of support in real time. I think I'm too preoccupied with myself to have a relationship."

"So your answer to that problem isn't to pay more attention to me but to stop seeing me?"

Rand paused, silent, unable to answer. Shelley's tone had changed. She was no longer the shy, unassuming woman with a crush on her. She was a lawyer, scorned, pissed, and finally empowered. Rand looked up, felt proud of her, until she realized that wasn't the appropriate response.

"No answer?" Shelley asked, face red, jaw clenched. Rand held eye contact with her. "I fell in love with you."

Rand said nothing.

"I didn't hold anything back." Rand had thought Shelley adored her, but to hear it live was something different entirely. "You did and I was too naive to see it. My God, I'm a fool." Shelley unfolded her napkin and folded it again. "I'm emotionally stunted. When most people were going through this in their teens and twenties, I was hiding from myself." She put the napkin down on the table, set the fork and knife on it, lined it up. "I came out today."

Rand had looked away but yanked her head back, shocked. "What?"

Shelley had a weary smile on her face, a kind of resigned acceptance. "I was so excited to tell you. Or to have you just see it. I wrote a long article about being gay, my journey to God after growing up in an evangelical family. About my political ideology, my refusal to let go of personal liberty and freedom. I plan to write a book, too. It went up around two p.m. I'm sure it's breaking social media—like the kiss."

Rand sat forward, wanted to touch her, but Shelley pulled away. "I need to go." She yanked her purse from the chair and walked briskly from the restaurant. Rand was frozen, once again, but then stirred to life as Shelley passed by the window. Rand jumped up, chased out the door, and yelled at Shelley to stop.

Shelley turned at the end of the building and paused before the small alley leading to the parking lot. Rand walked toward her. "That is so brave," Rand said. "You will get so much attention, Shelley. Are you ready for it?"

"I'm more ready for that than I was for this. I thought you'd be with me." Then her tears came, and she turned away. Rand grabbed her arm, but Shelley shook her away. "I am so in love with you. I came here to be close to you. Just leave me alone, Rand." She fled. Dust from the asphalt sprayed up from the car's tires. Rand kept her car in sight until it turned around the corner from the traffic light closest to her.

CHAPTER TWENTY-THREE

Shelley curled up on her small sofa, pulled a blanket up over her head, and watched as Netflix counted down the next episode. She'd barely moved since she left Rand the night before. The idea of facing the world, with her announcement, without Rand, felt more overwhelming than she expected. She wasn't scared, or at least she didn't think that was the sensation settled on her chest like a python wrapped around her neck, squeezing.

Her phone lay in pieces on the kitchen floor. She threw it off the balcony in the middle of the night before, when Rand called her again and again, in a rare display of uncontrollable emotion. She'd already planned on taking a few days off work after the article posted to allow some of the noise to die down. She was a lesbian, formerly Evangelical, Republican. Shelley didn't think she needed to alter every world view she had about personal liberty, small government, and the free market to date other females. Apparently, Rand thought so. Wasn't that what she said?

Why did Rand break up with her? Did she do something wrong?

She put her feet on the floor. She'd not brushed her teeth or showered all day. This really took self-pity to a new level, but she had a broken heart. Her first broken heart, actually, at the age of thirty-one. Shuffling into the bathroom, she slipped off her too big T-shirt and underwear and leaned against the wall, watching the tub fill with water.

Shelley dropped a bath bomb in. She sunk into the tub up to her neck, and then went completely under the water. Shelley stayed there a few moments, the sounds of the world muffled by the water in her ears. When she came back up, she pushed stray wet hairs back from her face and reached for the towel hanging by the tub and dried her face.

She ran her hands down her body, over her breasts and stomach, and touched the tangle of dark hairs between her legs. She thought about how she'd dreamed of Rand doing the same, and then burst into tears, sobbing in the water, gasping for breath as she cried. She'd not cried for thirty years, and during the past year, felt as if it were her new state of being to do so at least every other day.

She'd been so naive to think Rand would love and accept her for exactly who she was, unlike her family. Republican or Democrat, humans demanded conformity and found ways to exclude no matter how liberal and open they professed to be.

Likely, Rand was flattered by her attention and lonely. She'd done nothing short of throwing herself on Rand. Shelley watched droplets of water crawl down the wall of the tub, closed her eyes, and thought about how it felt to hug Rand. Rand was a little shorter than her, smaller, but she felt so safe and protected in her arms. The invisible python tightened its grip on her neck.

She drifted further into her rumination, until banging on the door startled her. She splashed, leaped from the bath, and almost slipped on the floor.

She put on her robe, a few long strides taking her to the door. She peered through the peephole, and pulled back, aghast. It was her mom and dad. Shelley leaned her head against the door, turned away, and looked at her cell phone in pieces on the counter. They likely called, but given her temper tantrum, she wouldn't know. Another knock shook the door, and she felt embarrassed for herself and wary of her neighbors.

She hit the door, in response, and again, uncharacteristically, yelled. "Give me five minutes and stop pounding on the door." Murmured voices acknowledged her, and she moved into the bedroom, slipped on clothing quickly, and dried her hair enough to pull it back. She then took time to brush her teeth. Then, Shelley folded the blanket on the couch. Satisfied with the minimalist tidiness of her small apartment, she unlocked the chain and twisted the door handle.

"Hi, Mom and Dad," she said, a new confidence settling on her shoulders, even as the Rand python wrapped around her neck. The two states of being were confusing, but she was comfortable in confusion and cognitive dissonance. This thought made her giggle.

"Shelley," her father said, his face ashen and pulled. "You need to come home and let us help you." Her mom wept openly. "You've just traveled too far away from the loving embrace of your family and Jesus."

Shelley looked back and forth at them. It was nuts, really. All of it. Wasn't it possible to be gay and religious? Couldn't she have a relationship with God and another female? Her experience in the church in Manhattan reassured her she could. But she didn't want to argue about it because their minds were made up, just like Rand's mind was made up.

Everyone had an opinion about what was possible for her, and she was sick of it.

They were also her parents, so she stepped aside and invited them in. It felt better than having them stand on the stairs, talking about Jesus. Her mom came forward and collapsed on her couch in a histrionic fit of tears. Shelley watched with practiced, detached analysis. Her father stood right next to her and stepped into her personal space, hands on her shoulders. The heavy shadows in his eyes attached to the sadness inside her, and she leaned forward into his arms. He hugged her, and for a moment, she forgot to keep her distance. She just wanted him to fix everything for her.

"Shelley," her dad said, "please, sweetheart. For me. Come home so we can help you."

"How?" Shelley stepped away from him. She felt reckless. What did she have to lose? Nothing really. If she was finally open about who she was, secrets were meaningless and no one had power over her any longer. If she was open-hearted, it was harder to be hurt by judgment. Somewhere along the way, she stopped relying on them to validate her external reality, and that had made her so much harder to control. As this new understanding clicked into place, even heartbroken, Shelley found new inner space to rest upon.

"Really?" His tone sharpened. "Are you really asking how? You've betrayed God's law. Your mom is right. I was too indulgent."

"Oh," Shelley said. "So, this is all about you." Just like it was all about Rand. Fury replaced sadness. "I used to want to die. I'd think about all the ways I could kill myself. Did you know that? Do you care? Because you told me there was something wrong with me." Her dad looked conflicted, strained. How confusing and revolting dogmatic religion made the world. How could she argue with them when they were convinced their actions came from love? "There is nothing wrong with me. I can be who I am and still know God."

"That's liberal propaganda," he said. "It is not God's law and you know it."

"Fake news," Shelley shouted and then began to laugh. "And I don't like Trump. He's a terrible Republican. You should be ashamed you voted for him and you don't denounce him." She laughed harder, sadness and exasperation welling to a head inside her. She sat at the kitchen table and put her face in her hands. She should have anticipated a confrontation with her parents. How could she guess they'd fly four hours from Atlanta?

"I'm glad you find this amusing," her mom said.

"Not really," Shelley conceded. "I'm pretty overwhelmed."

"You need to ask Jesus for help," her mom said through tears. Shelley dropped her head on the table and put her arms over her head.

There was another knock. "Who the hell is that?" Shelley imagined it would be Rand, to really add to the Lifetime movie drama of the moment.

"Oh, so now we swear too," her mom said with more tears.

Shelley opened the door. It was Rachel, wearing scrubs. She was so beautiful and Shelley was so relieved she hugged her. Rachel held her.

"Are you okay?" Rachel asked as she let go of her. "And, well, there are other people here."

"Rachel, meet my parents." Shelley swept her hand around the room. Shelley said to her mother, "She made sure they got my appendix all the way out. Saved my life."

"It was a really angry appendix," Rachel said, making eye contact with Shelley's mom and dad. "Nice to meet you all." Then she turned to Shelley. "Do you want me to go? Or stay?"

"Stay," Shelley said immediately. "Don't go." Rachel moved to stand to the left of her.

"So what's going on?" Rachel tucked her hand in the crook of Shelley's arm and pulled her closer. As she did, Shelley's heart rate slowed, the python lessened its grip, and she felt almost normal for the first time in twenty-four hours.

"They read my article," Shelley said, though that was probably obvious to Rachel.

"It was quite the article," Rachel said with a smile, pulling away from Shelley to look at her with admiration. "I read it three times. Fucking awesome. You're a brave and beautiful being." Shelley began to cry, and Rachel put her arm around her waist.

Then, Rachel said, looking at Shelley's parents, "What are you thinking? Maybe we can grab an early dinner? I'm starving. I was coming to see if Shelley wanted to eat."

"Yes," Shelley said. "Please.

"Yeah?" Then Rachel turned to Shelley's parents. "Will you all join us?"

"I'd rather talk with my daughter," Shelley's dad said. "We flew here this morning from Atlanta. Cross-country. To see her and talk to her and bring her home."

"Okay, well, if that is what Shelley wants I can get behind it. But it's 2018, and Shelley is thirty-one, right?"

"Right," Shelley said.

"And since we live in America, and not some creepy theocracy where fathers own their daughters, well, I guess it's really up to her." Shelley looked at her with awe and gratitude.

"This is ridiculous. Shelley, have your friend leave so we can talk," Shelley's mom said.

"No. I appreciate you came all this way out of what you believe is love. I think it's more about you than me, and that's fine. But this isn't changing, I'll come home to visit if you want, but I'm right where I want to be. I'm sorry you wasted the money."

Her dad stood in front of her, hands at his sides, frozen. Shelley made eye contact with him and began to cry. His own pain and disappointment was obvious as he turned to leave. Shelley watched her mother, saddened, and touched her mom's arm. Her mom paused momentarily and then walked away. Shelley watched the door shut with more sadness than the day began. She wiped the tears streaming freely down her face.

"How did you know?"

Rachel pulled tissues from the box to hand to her. "I didn't. Rand told me what happened, I read your article, and I was worried about you. I tried texting and calling, but you didn't answer." Rachel picked up the pieces of Shelley's phone. "Well, I guess I know why."

"I was really angry," Shelley said.

"Yeah, Rand is acting like an asshole." Rachel sat next to Shelley on the couch and rubbed her back in slow circles. "Well, how about we go eat? Stop at the Apple store for a new phone?"

"Have you slept?"

"I'm fine. I'm off for four days now so I need to stay up until at least seven, get my clock reset," Rachel said, stretching her legs, hand resting just below Shelley's neck. "I want french fries. Deep fried french fries. And other fried things."

"I think that sounds perfect." Shelley said. "Let me get dressed."

❖

"Don't judge me. I've not eaten in twenty-four hours." Rachel finished her Diet Coke and ate more fries.

"Look how chubby I am. Really, do you think I judge a deep fried binge?"

"You're beautiful," Rachel said, sipping the refilled Diet Coke the server set on the table. "So, Rand."

"Yeah." Shelley waited.

"I think she's addicted to being miserable and guilty, which is what I told her. So, I'll tell you that."

"I shouldn't have drafted that lawsuit," Shelley said, taking a drink of her soda. She had no appetite.

"No," Rachel reassured her. "Come on. You were so kind to offer. Don't internalize this. This is all Rand, not that it makes a difference to how you feel."

"I'm really in love with her," Shelley shared, unable to look at Rachel.

"I know. The thing is, Shelley, she is too. She's just really depressed and has been. She will wake up." Shelley felt new hope forming around the edges of her perception. But then retreated from it. Her heart couldn't take any more ambivalence and confusion from Rand. "You don't need to wait, or give her time, or talk to her, but I think if you did, it would be okay. She's been trying to get a hold of you. Panicked. But she doesn't want to violate your boundaries."

"Did she send you?"

"God no. This is all my own doing. Obviously, I'm not concerned with your boundaries." Rachel ate more fries and pointed to the basket in the middle of the table. "Eat."

Shelley took another drink of her soda and thought about eating but couldn't. Rachel's eyes were sad and kind, and she patted Shelley's hand.

"You're fucking amazing," Rachel said, holding eye contact. "One brave woman. For writing that article. For breaking from a controlling evangelical religion, and then charting your own course, politically, socially, and personally. You're most brave for falling in love. Not all of us are brave enough to do any of that." She rubbed Shelley's hand and then withdrew to her side of the booth.

"Should I call Rand?"

"What do you want to do?"

Shelley folded her hands in her lap and looked around the restaurant. "Go to New York for a few days. Get out of town while my family is here. Decide how I feel."

"Then let's do that. I'll give you a ride to the airport." Rachel pointed at the server bringing their food. "As soon as I eat. I need fuel."

"Thank you. I don't know how I'll ever repay you," Shelley said.

"Be my friend. We're good," Rachel said.

CHAPTER TWENTY-FOUR

R and put her elbows on her desk. Her final patient of
the day didn't arrive. She was considering wrapping
up for the day when a bird struck the window. She watched it
slide down the glass before dropping to the ground. She raced
from the office, slamming the door closed behind. Her feet
echoed in the stairwell, and her heart felt like a lead weight
that dropped again and again in her chest.

Rand pressed the long metal bar across the industrial door
with her forearm and elbow and rushed through the rocks to
see if the bird was still alive. It was a small dove, gray-beige in
color, and Rand stood over it and watched its eyes blink, open
and closed. One wing bent at an angle, and as Rand leaned
close, the bird tried to right itself and get away. Rand shushed
it, tried to calm it, and took off the long sleeve button-down
shirt she wore over a simple blue T-shirt. She wrapped the bird
in her shirt and cradled it in her arms.

She stepped from the rocks, not wanting to jostle the bird.
She walked silently and slowly through the lobby of her office
and stepped into the elevator to ride up one flight. Her patient
still had not arrived, so she gathered her keys and things and

walked back the route she just traveled. She started her car in route, hoping the air would cool some before she arrived.

Once in the car, she settled the bird gently in the passenger seat and dialed Rachel.

"Rand?" Rachel answered immediately.

"Can you save a bird? One flew into my window at the office and I think it broke its wing."

"I'm a human doctor," Rachel said this deliberately, directly, and Rand knew she was angry with her about Shelley.

"Rachel, come on."

"Take it to the wildlife center up in Paradise Valley."

Rand heard the television behind Rachel.

"Remember that time we x-rayed the squirrel at the hospital and you set its leg and took it home with you?" She heard Rachel shifting on the other side of the phone. "I know you're mad at me for Shelley."

"You were irresponsible and broke her heart." Her tone was so direct Rand flinched.

"I know. It's not the bird's fault." Rand imagined Rachel on the other side of the phone, weighing the choice to help her. "Rach, come on."

"Fine. Meet me at the animal clinic next to the hospital. My friend Julie owns the place."

"I love you," Rand said.

"I don't like you much right now," Rachel answered tersely.

"Right," Rand said, putting the car in reverse. "Me and the dove are on our way."

❖

Rand moved deliberately through town, weaving in and out of traffic, one hand on the bird in the front seat. She pulled into the parking lot of the animal clinic about twenty minutes after hanging up the phone with Rachel. Rachel waited by her car, arms crossed over her chest. Rand parked next to her and put the dove into Rachel's outstretched hands.

Together, they walked into the clinic and into the back room. Rachel placed the small dove on a steel table and a technician stood next to her, watching. Rachel cupped the dove with one hand and gently lifted its wing, and then felt along its body. The bird blinked at her, attempting to move away but unable to do so. Rachel's face darkened with sadness.

"What?"

"I think her neck is broken." Rachel moved the bird gently on the table, trying to elicit an appropriate response, and the technician agreed. Rachel wrapped the bird back up in Rand's shirt and put her hand over it gently. She met Rand's eyes. "I think the best thing we can do is put her down."

"No," Rand said, moving to take the bird from Rachel.

Rachel put both hands on Rand's shoulders and met her eyes directly. "Stop." Rand stopped. "We'll take care of it. Go outside and wait for me." Rand did as she was told.

Rand waited outside in the late afternoon heat and there were tears on her cheeks. The sound of a car door slamming across the parking lot and the roar of the car wash across the street settled into the background of the moment, as an airplane moved across the sky, adjusting its trajectory and descent for Sky Harbor airport.

Rand put her hand on her stomach and dry heaved.

Shocked, she stumbled to her car and fumbled for her keys. Another heave struck her. She stopped at the trash can by the pillar and threw up. Though disgusted by the idea of touching the trash can, it gave her balance as she threw up more. Somehow, Rand gained enough control to open the car door and start the engine. Rachel found her a few minutes later, half in and half out of her car, hands on her knees.

When she felt Rachel's hands on her shoulders, Rand began to cry, and her body shook from the shock of expulsion. She and Shelley were not so different after all. Her singular capacity to repress emotions was destroyed by an onslaught of too much. Rachel led Rand to her car and drove her the few blocks to her apartment. Rand sat with her feet pulled up under her in the front seat, head on the window, as her nausea abated.

Rand followed Rachel compliantly. Inside Rachel's apartment, Rand sat on the couch and took water from Rachel, with two pills she swallowed without question. Rachel sat next to her.

"What did I just take?"

"Zofran and Xanax," Rachel said.

"I don't even want to know why you have those readily available," Rand said.

"I have my own issues," Rachel said.

The Xanax settled into her limbs and relaxed her central nervous system. Rand's jaw loosened. Her hands tingled. Rachel turned on the television.

"Did the bird really die?"

"It did. But it was kind of you to try and save it," Rachel said.

"I didn't want it to die," Rand said.

"I know." Rachel smoothed back her hair. "I think you'll feel better if you cry."

"Why do you think I puked?"

"Because the immensity of everything hit you and I don't think you could handle it anymore."

"You're so smart and pretty," Rand said. "I love you."

"You're high," Rachel said. "Know who else is smart and pretty?"

"Shelley," Rand said, covering her face with her hands. "Oh my God, Shelley. What did I do?"

"I don't really know," Rachel said. "But we'll figure it out later." An episode of a serial killer drama played on the television, the soothing presence of her friend and the welcome relief of Xanax made her believe, for the first time since Kim died, that anything was possible.

CHAPTER TWENTY-FIVE

Tony was in London for a three-month play when Shelley arrived in New York. She missed him terribly, and they FaceTimed for three hours her first night at his apartment. She cried about Rand and her parents. He read her article out loud, dramatic and evocative, called it a celebration of her, his gay Republican. Just as Rachel's support helped her breathe again, Tony's friendship loosed the grip of the python around her neck.

She spent the first few days wandering, counting steps and struggling to find the ground beneath her feet. Shelley was shocked and surprised by the coverage of her article and spent a few hours every day on social media, reading comments. Everyone had something to say about it. Some gay organizations welcomed her out of the closet while others said she had a long road to redemption. Gay conservatives messaged her privately, thanking her, while gay liberals messaged, telling her she had to pick a side. It was an either/or time, and Shelley found herself right in the middle of it.

There was a text from Rand waiting on her phone, a simple request for a phone call, but she wasn't ready for it. It was naive and foolish to assume Rand felt as she did. She'd missed all the signs that said Rand wasn't available. She was so taken with Rand's confidence and certainty. Shelley was so physically attracted to her, everything else was drowned out by the roar of desire. Shelley's selective blindness was only visible with distance, and as she looked across the Hudson, her heart broke with the realization that Rand didn't love her. She walked home, meandering through the streets, adrift, nerves shaken.

That night, Shelley's phone rang at two a.m.

"Hello?" Sleep had not been regular or steady, but she'd drifted off a few hours before.

"Shelley." It was her mom.

"Mom?"

"It's Noah." Her younger brother.

"What's wrong, Mom?"

"He's gone, Shelley. An aneurism they think."

Shelley didn't understand and scrambled to turn on the light. She thought it would help. "What do you mean? Is he okay? Is he in the hospital?"

"No," her mom said. "He's gone."

Shelley sat on the couch. The light hurt her eyes and she regretted turning it on. She should just turn it off again, go back to sleep, wake up, never answer the phone again. Pack up, head back to Phoenix. Had she left enough water and creamer in the fridge for Tony, or should she run downstairs to the bodega to pick up more? She should tidy up the apartment too, just to be certain it was nice for him.

"Shelley?" She was on the phone with her mom. What had her mom said?

"Mom," Shelley said. "I don't understand."

"Can you come home?"

Why should she go home? It would be awful at home. Her parents and family couldn't love her because she was gay. She wanted to talk to Rand. Why was Rand so far away?

"Yeah," Shelley finally said, struggling back into her body. There was a siren outside. Did someone call the paramedics for Noah? She covered her mouth with her hand. Noah was dead. She had to go home. "I'll be there as soon as I can."

❖

Shelley had heard about dissociation upon learning of someone's death but didn't truly understand it until she walked through the motions of getting to her family the next day in a haze of unreality. Time stilled in moments, here and there, her consciousness split apart by the stark, empty realization of death. Car engines were louder. The birds moved slower in flight against the orange hue of the rising sun. The security line at the airport was surreal.

Waiting at the gate for her plane, Shelley watched a young couple kiss and hug. She wanted to do that with Rand. Wanted to feel young and free. Wanted to forget about the heaviness of guilt, obligation, and the weight of expectations. Wanted to flee mortality. Loving despite the certainty of death was the most absurd human behavior, and she wanted to participate in it. Shelley wanted to be alive.

She texted Rand. A simple message. Told her what happened. Where she was going. Then, she turned off her phone, put it in her bag, and boarded the plane.

❖

Her oldest brother, Asher, waited at curbside pick up. There was a text from him when she powered up the phone after the plane landed. There were many others, but she was saddened not to see one from Rand. Rachel and Jamie both texted and asked for the address to send flowers. She sent it quickly, tucking away her disappointment at not hearing from Rand.

She tossed her bag into the trunk of his car and buckled her seat belt as he pulled away from the curb, silent. They'd not spoken since the fall before, and not at all since she published her article.

"How are Mom and Dad?" Shelley broke the silence. She counted light poles as they drove.

"As expected," he said. He'd not looked at her.

"Asher," Shelley said. "I know it's been a while since we've talked. I'm sorry for that."

"Just don't make this any harder on our parents," he said. "You've already done enough."

"All I did was be honest about who I am," Shelley said.

"And break their hearts. All of us. You betrayed us," Asher said.

"That's ridiculous and you know it," Shelley said. "I agonized over this decision. I spent months in therapy. It was so hard. I knew you'd all view it that way, but it's not what it was. I had to be me."

"That's liberalism for you. Everything is about worship of the self, individualism. You do you. Psychology makes us all selfish. We justify carnal desires by talking about 'self-truth' and identity we like to think is subject to change. Gender swapping. Same sex marriage. All a violation of God's law and you know it because you grew up the same way as me."

Shelley sighed and rested her chin in her hand. She'd counted almost three hundred light poles and decided to give it up.

"I don't want to argue. How is it possible for us to move forward together? As brother and sister? Especially given what's happened," Shelley said.

"You can repent," Asher said.

"This is why America is so divided," Shelley said. "How can we move forward together if one side truly believes we're an abomination and won't give? Do you have any idea how damaging that is? To tell me to repent? How much it hurts?"

Asher didn't respond. His certainty felt as fixed as Rand's, who still had not texted her back. They drove in silence. Shelley was done trying to justify her existence and beliefs. She was done trying to get others to understand how it was possible to be gay and believe in small government, personal liberty, and God. She wasn't going to chase after Rand any longer. Life ended. Noah was dead. She was aging. Her parents were aging. Rand's partner died. Everyone and everything alive would die one day.

Despite this, humans found ways to fight and alienate each other, caught up in the power of their rationalizations to avoid their finitude. Modern tribes clashed, powered by ancient DNA that kept early Homo sapiens safe from the other. In the other, we saw ourselves and were afraid. Host and hostile. Caught between a desire to welcome the other and destroy the other, humans struggled to compartmentalize the noisy confusion of a changing, connected world. They projected their worst fears on one another.

Asher stopped at a stop light and put both hands on the wheel, twelve and three o'clock.

"Shelley," he said. "I don't know how to handle any of this."

Shelley unbuckled her seat belt and hugged him. She held his head on her shoulder, remembered summers at the lake house, chasing through the woods together. Saw the stones he skipped across the water, and thought that love should be enough, but it never was. He grabbed her arm with his big hand and cried with her, until the sound of a car horn behind them gave him no choice but to move.

They arrived at her parents' house, distraught and emotional, and walked in holding hands. Shelley's mother enveloped her in a hug. Her father did the same, her other siblings following after. They sat in silence in the front room, Shelley's nieces and nephews huddled together in groups, coloring and drawing, silent. Their confused expressions drew Shelley to them. She sat on the floor and they congregated around her, climbing in her lap.

Her parents spoke of plans for services. Shelley shifted her niece on her lap and used her phone to book a hotel room. Rachel texted again, checking in, and Shelley sent her the hotel information, told her she'd be there until she returned to New York. There was still no message from Rand, and though Shelley didn't believe her grief could intensify, it did. Perhaps it was her fault. She'd fled Phoenix, despite Rand's efforts to reach her. The enormity of all her losses piled on, and she cried again, remembering Noah's texts of support. His phone call after the picture was released, as he tried to warn her.

Why hadn't she reached out more often to him? He was young, enthralled by his life at the university. They'd spoken enough, given where they both were in life. Now, on this side of tragedy, nothing would ever be enough.

Evening came, with dinners served by church members. They hugged her, welcomed her home, and said nothing about her revelation. She'd known many of them her whole life. Shelley read their discomfort but didn't press. It wasn't the time for a conversation about the spiritual and psychological implications of Christianity and homosexuality. It was a time to grieve. But she appreciated their kindness and warmth, nonetheless. Death gave them all an opportunity to choose what they saw and what mattered, at least in those moments.

Shelley excused herself about eight p.m. and waited for her Uber on the sidewalk. She turned to look at her parents' house and remembered being there last fall. Her ride arrived and she climbed in, not saying good-bye. She'd see everyone the next day. Tonight, she needed sleep. She closed her eyes in the back seat and was jostled awake when the driver hit the brakes and said, "We're here."

Shelley thanked him, dragging her bags behind her. A heavy tired settled on her then, forlorn darkness. Her younger brother died. Rand wasn't texting back. She was an out lesbian who worked for a Libertarian think tank. Earlier in the day, for distraction, she browsed the memes that had cropped up in recent weeks with her name on them. They ranged from unkind to objectifying. Someone had photoshopped her face, about ten pounds heavier, onto the Republican elephant.

Shelley's walk to reception to check in felt unending.

"Shelley." She heard but chose to ignore the call. It was probably someone who wanted to thank her or deride her, and there was no energy for any of it. "Shelley," came again and then a warm hand was on her arm. She turned away from the clerk.

"Rand," Shelley said. "What are you doing here?"

"I came for you," Rand said, and then pulled her into a hug, arms around her waist. Shelley wrapped her arms around Rand's neck and hung on like a tide would sweep her away if she let go.

CHAPTER TWENTY-SIX

Rand saw Shelley dragging her suitcases like they weighed thousands of pounds. She looked so tired and worn. The trauma of her brother's death hung around her like a shroud. The weight of such tragedy could suffocate her if she didn't process it. Rand called for her twice before approaching her. She'd spent all day in transit, taking the first flight she could get out of Phoenix. It took her to Chicago, where she boarded a plane to Atlanta, almost three hours later. Rachel had texted her Shelley's hotel address. Rand was going to text, tell her she was coming, but she was afraid Shelley would tell her to stay home.

Shelley finished checking in, and Rand took their bags in hand. She followed Shelley to the elevator and they rode up together in silence. The doors opened on Shelley's floor. A group of teenagers waited. They pushed on as Rand and Shelley tried to get off.

"You can wait for us to get off. The elevator won't go anywhere," Rand said, concerned about Shelly.

"Hey, aren't you that gay Christian?" the girl spoke.

It was the boy's turn next. "Fuck yeah, she is. I saw you on the news."

Rand nudged Shelley forward, hand on the small of her back. "Come on," she said. "What room is it again?"

"Six nineteen," Shelley said, energy waning.

Rand found the room and took the card from Shelley's hand. She opened the door for her and set the suitcases in the corner of the room.

"Why don't you rest for a while?" Rand went into the bathroom and came back with a wet washcloth. She wiped Shelley's face and neck, and then tossed it toward the bathroom. Rand touched Shelley's face, and then held it with the palm of her hand. She shifted forward, bending to rest her forehead on Shelley's. "I'm so sorry," Rand said. Shelley collapsed into Rand's arms.

She shifted so they could face each other on the bed. Rand kissed her forehead, nose, and cheek. "You look so tired," Rand said. Shelley put her arms around Rand's waist and held her close, face burrowed in her neck now.

"I'm so tired," she said.

"I know," Rand said. "Try to sleep a bit."

"Don't go," Shelley said. "Can you stay?"

"Yes," Rand said. "I'll stay." Shelley turned to her side, nestled her back against Rand. Shelley fell asleep almost instantly. Her fatigue was palpable. So much had happened in her life, in such a short amount of time, she must be overloaded like a circuit breaker powering too many lights. Losing someone close to you was traumatic, no matter the circumstances. Shelley had spoken about her brother Noah on more than one occasion. It was obvious she adored him.

When Rand saw Shelley's text, the first in two weeks, her instinct had been to find her. About a week after she left town, Rand became frantic, desperate, and wanted to chase her. Rachel told her to give Shelley a little time and space. It seemed prudent. But all that disappeared when she learned what happened. It was on the news in Chicago while she waited for her connecting flight. The news anchors talked about Noah's death in between quips about the family's politics. Rand supposed it was inevitable, but hoped Shelley was avoiding the news.

Was it really possible to love someone so quickly? Rand watched Shelley sleep. Her face was peaceful in rest. Her dark eyelashes twitched with a dream. Rand held her hand, on her hip, and was overwhelmed with a desire to take care of her.

She'd been such an ass. But it wasn't intentional. Shelley captivated her, right from the start. There was something about her. Rand wasn't ready for a relationship when they first met, but wasn't willing to let her get too far away, either. Shelley was right to flee. Rand pulled her forward and pushed her away, again and again. So many conflicting signals. It was the hot and cold game she lectured her patients about, and here she was, doing it to this extraordinary woman.

It didn't matter they disagreed philosophically about the role of government in their lives. It didn't matter Shelley believed in God. What mattered was how they could show up for each other. What mattered was that they never ran out of things to talk about. Rand nestled against Shelley, shared her pillow, and her hair fell against her face. She breathed it in.

It was more than enough. What they had was more than enough to get through anything. If Rand could just let it begin.

❖

Rand woke alone on the bed. Light filtered in through the heavy beige drapes. It was six in the morning. She'd slept through the night and hadn't felt Shelley rise. The shower ran in the bathroom. A few moments later, the water turned off. Rand listened to the noises on the other side of the wall, imagined Shelley drying off, dressing, wrapping her hair in a towel. The door opened, mist billowed out, and then there was Shelley, as Rand imagined.

"Good morning," Shelley said. She dressed in slacks and a blouse. Her hair was pulled up, and she wore no makeup.

"Hi," Rand said. "How do you feel?" Shelley stared at her but said nothing. "Shelley?"

"Why did you come?"

Rand shifted off the bed and scooted past her to use the bathroom. She rinsed her face and brushed her teeth with the complimentary toothbrush. When she came back, Shelley was in the chair by the window. The drapes were open, and Rand was surprised to see so much green.

"I came because I care," Rand said. "Because I'm an ass." She sat on the edge of the bed, across from Shelley. "I'm sorry, for your brother, your family. I'm sorry for what I did and how I've behaved."

"Thank you," Shelley said, still watching her, guarded. "I appreciate last night. I was really upset."

Rand's gaze drifted out the window. She'd flown to Atlanta to be near Shelley. Chased her across the country. It was now or never. So Rand went to Shelley, knelt down in front of her, and cupped her face in her hands. Rand pulled her forward, kissed her, and when Shelley didn't pull away, she kissed her again. Shelley wrapped her arms around her neck, hand in her hair and held her, mouth barely open, lips firm.

"Rand," she said. Rand felt the depth of her emotion just as she did at the food truck event, but she didn't pull away. She eased into it, dropped her hand to Shelley's waist, and pulled her closer. "Don't push me away again. If you do this. I can't stand it again."

"I promise. I won't. Give me a second chance. Let's start again," Rand said. Shelley kissed her again, body pressed against her, and Rand responded, not afraid. Shelley was so soft and pliant in her arms, her lips felt like velvet. Why had she resisted?

The phone rang and Rand pulled away but didn't retreat. Shelley touched her face and ran her thumb across her mouth.

"Do you want to get that?" Rand pointed at the phone. Shelley nodded. Rand handed her the phone.

"Hi, Mom," Shelley said. Rand sat on the bed again. Shelley was silent, listening. Rand heard a voice but couldn't make out the words. "Okay. I'll head over in a bit. Just let me know what else I can do." Rand searched for her own phone and checked text messages. She let Rachel and Jamie know they were okay. "I love you, too, Mom," Shelley said as she hung up.

"I don't need to keep you, Shelley. I know there is a lot going on," Rand said.

"I can't believe you came," Shelley said.

"I can't believe it took me this long to get my act together," Rand said. "I just wanted you to know you're not alone."

"Are you staying or, well, what's your plan?"

"I don't want this be about anything other than your brother. I came to ask you to come home when this is done," Rand said. "I came to ask for a second chance."

"The next few days are going to be so busy," Shelley said. "I think I'm in shock."

"Likely," Rand said. "I've got to head back today. I have patients booked all day tomorrow. I moved everyone to make my mad cross-country dash."

"It was exceptionally gallant of you," Shelley said with a smile. Rand grinned but was overcome with sadness when she considered the circumstances.

"So you'll come home?"

"Home," Shelley said. "To Phoenix."

"Yeah," Rand said. "Please. At least for now."

"All my stuff is there anyway," Shelley said.

"And there are a lot of libertarians," Rand said.

"I've heard," Shelley said with a smile.

CHAPTER TWENTY-SEVEN

The auditorium was filled to capacity. Shelley hid in the far back corner. The past few days were a blur of family and church events. Her body was heavy with grief. The media had interwoven the narrative of her coming out with her brother's unexpected death. It left her feeling conflicted and confused. Maybe Asher was on to something. Maybe the modern world's indulgence of the individual above all else was selfish. But in the absence of self-actualization, what was there? Once basic needs were met, like food, clothing, shelter, it was all that was left.

It's why it was a modern world problem. There were always queer humans. Indigenous people called them Two-Spirits. It's just that the struggle to find food, warmth, and avoid sickness gave them little time to ponder their inner world. Shelley watched a young mother adjust a child on her lap while controlling two who sat next to her. Humans arrived in the twenty-first century with worldviews formed five thousand years before penicillin. Those world views were clashing with new understanding of sciences and psychology. The outer and the inner, dancing for realignment, everyone struggling to maintain what they thought mattered most for human survival.

Shelley looked for a chair, her head swimming. She wished it were possible to power down her thoughts, not see so much, but knew it wasn't. There were twenty-seven pictures on the wall. What was Rand doing? She pulled out her phone to check for a text. There wasn't one. She shifted her suit jacket and then flinched at a flash. A reporter took her picture. In the middle of her brother's funeral service. The choir sang. Then she was mad.

She left the chair and walked to the reporter, strides strong and confident. Shelley yanked the camera from his hands and threw it on the ground. The sound was muffled by the rug it fell on.

"It's my brother's funeral," Shelley said.

"You'll pay for that," he said.

"Send me a bill," Shelley said and returned to her seat. That would make the news too. She was fairly certain someone else snapped a picture of it. There were cameras everywhere. No one was allowed a dramatic moment of emotion without being held accountable for it forever. No one was allowed anything other than perfection. Shelley thought life might have been simpler if she could travel back in time to live in a convent without running water. It just needed a large library and garden. A small barn with animals and many dogs. No cameras.

And Rand. It definitely needed Rand.

❖

The picture of Shelley smashing a reporter's camera was on social media within the quarter hour. She looked at it while riding in the limo to the graveside. Her father was next to her. They'd barely spoken since she arrived home. She closed her eyes and leaned her head back against the seat of the car.

"What's that?" It was her dad. He took her phone from her hands.

"I smashed a camera," Shelley said.

"You're full of surprises these days," he said.

"Tell me about it," Shelley said and took her phone back. "It's not a very flattering angle. I need to get back to the gym."

"What did he do?"

"Took my picture during the hymn. Flash right in my eyes. I was angry. It's Noah's funeral," Shelley said.

"Jesus once turned over tables in the temple, remember?"

"I do feel morally justified," Shelley said. "Also concerned about my mental health and emotional regulation."

Her dad laughed, lightly. No one else in the car joined their conversation. They drifted into comfortable silence, like family can when words run out and there was just enough love to allow it.

"I don't understand, Shelley," he finally said. "I don't think any of us do."

"There is nothing to understand," Shelley said. "It's who I am. I am who I've always been, Dad."

"I keep thinking about seeing Noah two weeks ago when I was in Lynchburg. We went to lunch. I'll never take him to lunch again." He wiped tears from his eyes. Shelley reached for his hand, overcome by emotion. She leaned her head against his shoulder. Her mom and sister cried.

"I don't want to not have lunch with you again," he said to Shelley. "Not talk about books."

"We can still do that, Dad. I'm gay. Not dead," Shelley said. "You taught me that we wrestle with God. We wrestle with the things we can't explain easily, and from that struggle, we draw our faith and find love and hope."

Her dad shifted and put his arm around her shoulder, chin on her head. The car was silent, nothing resolved, but possibility present.

❖

The day was finally over. Shelley lay on her back on the hotel bed. There were seven stains on the ceiling, and she couldn't fathom their origin. There was an email from MSNBC. They wanted her to join Greg to talk about coming out and her brother's death. Gay relations with Evangelical Christianity and the Religious Right, and anything else. Greg followed up individually, with condolences. He also asked her to promise not to break his cameras, in an attempt to make her smile. It worked.

She texted Rand about the invitation. She'd fly back to Manhattan, do the interview, and then return to Phoenix. If she wanted to gain some control over her public persona, it was necessary. Her only concern was that Rand would be upset. But she wasn't. Her response came almost immediately. Rand asked her to schedule it for next Monday, so she could join her. There was enough time to clear a few days on her calendar.

The idea that Rand would fly to New York City to support her was thrilling. She was also nervous. Would they share a hotel room? After wanting Rand for so long, was she really going to get her?

CHAPTER TWENTY-EIGHT

Rand rushed through the airport, chasing to the gate before the plane left. One of her least appealing character traits was that she was always late. It wasn't intentional. It wasn't that she didn't care. It was just that time seemed like a pliable, flexible substance, subject to her momentary emotions. She kept a schedule for work and tried to be as punctual as Shelley for Shelley, but otherwise, Rand often lost hours.

She packed her bag the night before while Jamie sat in the middle of her bed, chatting with her. One of the beagles had chewed a corner of her suitcase while their attention was elsewhere. Rand wasn't angry. The beagles could do anything and she'd laugh at them. They were divine beings, manifest in furry forms, and her love was unconditional.

The alarm went off at five a.m. and she woke on time. But then she checked FaceBook with her coffee and saw a meme about Shelley from a popular gay rights group. It sent her on a FaceBook rampage. She chided the person who posted it about dehumanizing people who were different. Then she slipped into a Google meme hole, sliding all the way to the bottom of the pit.

Rand was horrified at what she'd seen. She understood the animosity people felt toward Shelley's father and her family organization. It was hard not to do so. Rand felt it too. But people she believed were allies were adding their own cruelness to the pot, stirring dysfunction. She supposed sooner or later someone would have to figure out a way to cross the divide. Such anger and hostility couldn't carry on forever. Maybe that should be her next research topic. Religion and sexuality. Maybe Shelley could help her. There had to be some bridges in thought where gays could meet with Christians in America and put a stop to the fight.

Rand knew it meant that people could be, just as they were, without fear of judgment, retaliation, and alienation. The Christian Right was clinging to an ideal that never existed. Family values was a caricature of what they believed America was like before the civil rights movements in the middle of the twentieth century. It wasn't real. There were still gay people. Still transgender people. They were rendered invisible. The way forward had to include visibility and acceptance, and it felt like a daunting task.

Rand scanned her ticket, lost in thought, and ambled up the plane walkway. She'd see Shelley in six hours. Kissing her in the hotel room and good-bye the day she dashed back to Phoenix had been mind-altering.

It was a revelation worthy of religious verse. But that probably wasn't the bridge in thought they needed to find to begin repairing relationships.

Rand buckled her seat belt, turned on Spotify, and slipped on her headphones. The plane lurched onto the runway, lights dimmed for takeoff. In the weeks since Rand chased Shelley away, her entire consciousness rebooted. Her brain was like a computer stuck in a restart update that finally lurched back to the home screen. Rand felt like she was back. The lawsuit's resolution allowed her to let go of the burning burden of her past. Kim would never really leave her. Her love carried her through the first few decades of her life. She would always be present in Rand's life and carried into every new chapter. She'd honor her memory by living well. It's what Kim would want.

To carry on after loss was bravery in real time. Rand told her patients that. Now she told herself it was okay to be unstuck. She could let go of all that she carried and move forward into a new relationship.

Shelley was waiting.

❖

Shelley waited by an LED advertisement board outside Terminal C at Newark International Airport. Her plane beat Rand's by forty-five minutes. Rand saw her before Shelley found her in the crowd. Rand paused, watching Shelley tuck a stray hair behind her ear. She wore a pair of jeans and a light sweater. It stretched tight across her breasts, and Rand flushed with desire. The arctic ice had melted.

"Shelley," Rand called, waving her arm. Shelley saw her, met her eyes, and tried to find a path to her through the crowd. "I'll come to you," Rand yelled, hands cupped. "Stay there."

Shelley smiled and waited. Rand found her way to her and circled her arms around Shelley's waist.

"I've missed you," Shelley said, lips against Rand's ear.

"Me too," Rand said. "Let's get out of here." Rand tugged her forward, arm around Shelley's waist. The air in Newark was heavy and wet. It was the best flight for the price on such short term, so an adventure of cabs or PATH trains waited for them to get into the city. They waited in line for a cab, not talking, in each other's arms. Someone took a picture of them, pointing at Shelley. The flash lit up the space, hidden from daylight by layers of cement.

"You ready for everyone to know?" Rand held on to Shelley's waist with more intention and turned to face her. "What if it doesn't work out, Shelley? Then we have to break up in public, too," Rand said.

"I rarely do something that isn't successful," Shelley said with a small grin. But her cheeks flushed.

"I'm messy and always late," Rand said.

"Are you chickening out?"

Was she? Rand searched inside for answers as their turn for a taxi came. She took Shelley's hand and put one hand on her face. She kissed her before they climbed in the cab and again once they were inside.

They had dinner at the same restaurant where they ate the year before. The server was different, but the food was the same. Their conversation was more intimate. They discussed Shelley's family, her brother's funeral, grief, and the road to recovery. Shelley cried and Rand joined her. They left the restaurant hand in hand and wandered the streets, stumbling onto a small hotel with vacancies. They gladly left their bags in the room before walking again. Night came and the lights of the city turned on.

Rand zipped her hoodie.

"Cold?" Shelley rubbed Rand's arms and then hugged her waist.

"I'm perpetually cold everywhere but Phoenix May through October," Rand said.

"It's chilly," Shelley agreed. "Since the sun went down." They stopped for coffee and sipped it as they wandered through the streets. Rand liked the warmth of Shelley at her side, how her hand felt in hers. She thought about kissing her again. If they kissed more than once, did that mean there was ongoing consent? She'd been with Kim for so long, the idea of touching Shelley was terrifying. What if her skills were not up to par? But Shelley was even more naive about it all than she was.

Jamie would tell her she was overthinking and to butch up. Rand giggled and Shelley turned to her.

"What?"

"I just had a funny thought," Rand said, smiling.

"Do you want to share?"

"Probably not," Rand said. "But it's nothing bad. I promise." Shelley stopped walking and stood in front of her, hands at her side. It looked like she wanted to say something.

"What?" Rand didn't move.

"I wanted you to know that I'm sorry I ran away," Shelley said.

"You don't need to apologize." Rand touched her arm and pulled her forward.

"I do," Shelley said.

"I told you I didn't want to spend time together anymore, that anything more than friendship wasn't possible." Rand was ashamed. "What else could you be expected to do?"

"You tried to reach out, though. When I didn't respond, I can't imagine how that felt," Shelley said.

"Awful. But I hurt you too." Falling in love could make a reasonable person behave like an idiot. "I'm just sorry," Rand said. "I knew when I met you here last year that I felt something, but I just wasn't ready."

"Neither was I," Shelley said. "Maybe I'm still not. I'm so scared. What if I mess this up? What if it doesn't work? What if you change your mind? I've not felt like this before."

"Neither have I," Rand said.

"But you were married," Shelley said. "I feel like—"

Rand cut her off. "I've never felt like this." It was direct and left no room for anything other than a literal interpretation. "Let's walk for a while," Rand said, taking her hand. "Tell me anything."

Time became malleable and Rand lost track of it. She told Rand about the conversation with her dad in the limo, her hope, and asked if Rand thought it was misguided. Rand told her hope never was, but should be managed, and shared her ideas about working together on a project to discuss the LGBTQ+ relationship with Christianity in America. Shelley admitted she no longer identified as Christian but found solace in the mystical God who transcended all religions.

On the street corner outside Times Square where Rand watched her drive away in the back seat of a cab, Rand gave her the only gift worthy of Shelley. It was the best apology Rand could imagine and the ultimate act of acceptance for someone like her to offer. It was the best she could do, and nervously, Rand hoped it was enough.

Rand took her wallet from her pocket and pulled out a white paper card.

"What's that?" Shelley smiled at Rand, sipping the coffee they stopped to buy. The noise of Times Square faded away. Rand turned on the phone's flashlight.

"It's my new voter registration card," Rand said. Shelley leaned closer to it. "I updated my party affiliation to Independent. For you. Because I've heard you too."

Shelley grabbed her, arms around her neck, and kissed her. Then she laughed, hysterically, in a way Rand had never seen before.

"You did not," Shelley said. Rand shrugged and laughed. "Now you can't vote in the primaries."

"It didn't matter last time anyway. I voted for Bernie and the establishment won. Look what happened. I mean, let's be clear, I'm never voting for a Republican," Rand said, laughing.

"Is this a symbolic gesture?"

"Totally," Rand said, laughing so hard it was tough to catch her breath.

"Well, I'll do it too," Shelley said.

"No, you won't," Rand said, arms around her waist, spinning her. "You won't."

"I will," Shelley insisted. "You watch. I don't think I quite fit in the party anymore, but..." she paused and Rand finished.

"Small government, personal liberty, low taxes, blah, blah, the market." Shelley laughed and tightened her arms around Rand's neck, touched her face, and kissed her again.

"Of course you're wrong," Rand said when Shelley finished kissing her.

"Can I take that kiss back?"

"Nope. It was freely given, in free association, like pollution and drugs that cause cancer," Rand said. "No regulations to oversee the taking back of kisses."

Rand kissed Shelley, earnest suddenly. "I hope we never get tired of arguing."

"Me too," Shelley said, kissing Rand again.

"I really like kissing you," she said, innocent desire in her eyes. "It's a new discovery."

"Like a new flavor of ice cream," Rand said.

"Or a vegan Indian restaurant," Shelley said.

"Let's go back to the hotel," Rand said. "You have to be at the station early."

❖

They'd booked a room with double beds when they checked in. Shelley told her Tony was subletting his apartment so she needed a place to stay. When they found the hotel and made the reservations, Shelley didn't say anything to stop her from making a single reservation, but Rand didn't want to make any assumptions.

Rand felt grungy after her cross-country trip and all day Manhattan adventure, and showered first. Shelley left the room to find ice and water as Rand stepped into the bathroom. Shelley was in the bathroom now. The blow dryer turned on. Long hair had to be a tremendous amount of work. Women had to buy the right shampoo, conditioner, and spray stuff to keep out tangles.

Rand shimmied under the covers in the bed farther from the bathroom. Hopefully, Shelley would come out of the bathroom and throw herself into bed so it wasn't necessary for her to make the first move. She pulled the sheet over her head and burrowed into the middle of the bed. Probably wasn't going to send the best signal if Shelley came out of the bathroom and saw it, but it was too late. The door opened, so Rand stayed where she was under the covers.

"Rand? Are you okay?" Shelley's voice was muffled by the covers. This was ridiculous, Rand thought. She was forty years old, but she felt like she was fifteen. In Shelley's presence, she regressed. It was definitely something to chew over in talk therapy with Mary.

Rand pulled the covers off her head and sat on the edge of the bed.

"Momentary lapse," Rand said. "A bit of panic. I'm fine. Nothing to worry about."

"Don't panic," Shelley said. "We don't, I mean, I want to, but there isn't any rush. We've both had so much going on. I mean, I'm nervous too…" Her voice trailed off, and she looked away, fumbling in her bag. Rand forgot her own self-consciousness. Shelley was just on the other side of the room, but she couldn't close the distance fast enough.

Rand pulled Shelley backward, into her arms, and kissed her neck. Shelley gasped and dropped the bottle into the bag. She turned around to face Rand and met her kisses.

"Shelley," Rand whispered. "Come to bed with me."

"Yes," Shelley said. They settled effortlessly together, legs intertwined.

Rand undressed her slowly, overcome with the desire to have her mouth on every inch of Shelley's body. As Rand did, she took comfort in her arms, and as she moved between her thighs, Shelley's desire for her overwhelmed any remaining hesitancy. Shelley moved with her, unguarded and open, vulnerable in a way only someone who'd never had a broken heart could be, and whispered Rand's name, in pleas and gasps. Rand leaned over her, arm under her head, lips pressed against Shelley's, feeling her way into Shelley's pleasure, watching her reactions, and then marveling as she found the rhythm that brought down all of Shelley's barriers.

At the peak of what should have taken her over the edge, Rand retreated, wanting her mouth on Shelley. Shelley cried out, confused and grasped Rand, desperate to keep her close, until she understood her intentions. Then, her anticipation swelled, and Rand's mouth on her created a ripple of sensation that overwhelmed her senses. From between her thighs, Rand held Shelley's hand as she cried out, her back arching, stomach quivering.

After, Rand rested with her head on Shelley's soft stomach, and then moved upward to shift her into her arms, back against her front, hands intertwined. Shelley kissed her fingers and then turned toward her, capturing her mouth again and again, soft kisses, hands on her face, legs intertwined. Shelley wanted to give Rand the same pleasure she'd just felt and pushed against her, uncertain but determined, and felt alive and powerful, with the thrill of Rand in her arms. The moonlight broke through the spaces between the window and the blinds, and their dance began again.

❖

Shelley's hand rested against the base of Rand's back. Rand was on her stomach, head resting on her folded arms. They held eye contact and Rand smiled. Shelley kissed her again, and Rand cupped Shelley's chin gently. The clock on the table said it was two thirty a.m. Rand flipped to her back, and Shelley snuggled in her arms, head on her shoulder, leg draped over her thigh.

"I didn't know my body was capable of any of that," Shelley said, holding Rand's hand.

"Mine either." Rand pulled Shelley closer. The sounds of New York filtered in through the window. Horns. Sirens. Voices. Rand barely noticed them. "I might have sprained my shoulder," Rand said. Shelley rubbed Rand's left shoulder. "No, the other one." They laughed together, and Rand buried her face in Shelley's neck.

"That tickles," Shelley said, pushing against Rand, who tickled her sides. They fell into more laughter until Shelley was on top of Rand, straddling her waist, pinning her arms above her head. "I'm stronger than you," Shelley said.

"I just let you win." Rand grinned. Shelley let go of Rand's arms and cupped her face, kissing her, alive with the still new sensation of Rand's mouth open beneath her own. Her arousal returned, and Shelley wondered at it, amazed. Her instinct was to try to analyze it, but she was too consumed to hold the thought for long. She pressed against Rand, finding the firm pressure between her thighs intoxicating. Rand grabbed her hips, sensing her intention, and Shelley gasped as the extra pressure ignited a deeper pleasure.

Shelley tipped her head back, hands on Rand's shoulders, and rocked back and forth tentatively and then opened her eyes to look at Rand, lips parted. Shelley closed her eyes, momentarily overwhelmed by how exposed she was, and thought about retreating. Rand put one arm around her waist, one hand on her hip, and pulled Shelley toward her as she half sat up in bed.

"I want you," Rand whispered in her ear. Shelley rocked against her in gasps and murmured pleas, as Rand held her, face to face, mouth to mouth. She was too aroused to worry any longer, and her earlier hesitation disappeared as she lost herself in the new sensation. Every nerve in her body burned.

Shelley's pleasure mounted, tears in her eyes, and as she fell into Rand's arms, she said, "I love you."

Rand rolled Shelley from on top, to her back, settling between her legs, mouth open on her neck, breasts, charting a path down her stomach. Shelley grabbed her hair, tugged her up, met her mouth.

"Rand," she said, vulnerable and scared.

"I love you," Rand said. "I'm madly, crazy in love with you, Shelley Whitmore."

"I'm considering that a binding contract," Shelley said and kissed her again. "I can't stop kissing you. Is that okay?"

"Um, I'll manage the burden of it," Rand said. Shelley kissed her. "I love you, did I mention that?"

CHAPTER TWENTY-NINE

I'm here with Shelley Whitmore, lawyer, political pundit, all-around extraordinary human," Greg said. "Should I add activist and camera breaker to the list?"

Shelley smiled. Her body pulsed with warmth from the night before with Rand. How did people who had good sex regularly concentrate when necessary? Maybe some of the newness of it would wear off, but she hoped not. She was nervous. That didn't normally happen. Rand kissed her cheek in the dressing room, having sensed it.

"You've had so much happen. Tragic, embarrassing, violating, good, and everywhere in between. Be kind to yourself." It was like talking to Taunya for all those months in Atlanta before finding the courage to be who she was. Rand's sensitivity was a gift, and she hoped to never take it for granted because it was rare.

"Well?" It was Greg. She'd not responded.

"He took my picture during my baby brother's funeral," Shelley said. Rand said her accent was stronger since visiting home. It sounded so even to her ears.

"That's a pretty valid reason," Greg said.

"Our social media culture is often vile, cruel, and inappropriate," Shelley said. "I find I've run out of tolerance for it."

"I don't disagree. Twitter is a battleground," Greg said. "I take it you've seen the memes out there about you."

"I have," Shelley said. "Anytime I'm miserable I can make it worse by reading memes about me."

"Why do you suppose there is so much animosity toward you?"

Shelley looked away from Greg and made eye contact with Rand, who stood behind him, off set. Rand waved at her.

"My family's church and organization takes an exceptionally strident position on LGBTQ+ matters. I think that position gives people very little room to react any other way to me," Shelley said. Greg was quiet, waiting. "I can't blame them. I understand. I love my family, my father means so much to me, so it's harder for me to be strident. But it became necessary for me to extract myself from them so I can make my own life. Be my own person."

"Be gay," Greg said.

"Well, I mean I've always been lesbian, but now I just need to be open about it," Shelley said.

"Of course," Greg said. "Will you stay Republican?"

"It's funny you ask." Shelley looked at Rand again. "When the party amends the platform to support gay marriage, ban conversion therapy, removes obstacles for transgender people to live and serve the country with dignity, and generally, takes a more conciliatory tone toward social issues and these hot topic cultural wars, I'll come back. I've been inspired to update my voter registration to Independent."

"Amazing," Greg said. "Where are you with the new progressive economic policies Democrats are pushing as we march toward the midterm?"

"I don't like anything that makes government bigger. It's not the answer," Shelley said. "I truly think I've settled into a more independent mindset. We need to take emergency action against climate change and preserve low tax liability so the free market can do its thing. The Republican Party needs to stop being a religious organization and get back to its Barry Goldwater roots. Democrats need to stop vilifying everyone who disagrees with them."

"What about the border and migration?"

"Invite me back to talk about that," Shelley said. "I don't have it in me today."

"What are you plans?"

"I started writing a book earlier this year. I'll finish that. Live my life. Mourn my brother. Look for opportunities to positively influence American political dialogue. I don't want to engage in polarizing behavior anymore."

"Are you involved with someone?" Greg smiled. He'd seen Rand earlier and made a grand show of taking credit for their relationship.

"I am," Shelley said. "But I'd like to keep it to myself for a while."

"I saw a picture of you at the airport," Greg said.

"So did I," Shelley said. "But that doesn't mean I have to talk about it."

"Do you think there's hope for America?"

"We have to find our way past this divisive rhetoric. We need leaders who unify us. Can get past these tribal impulses that pit us against each other. American ideals of justice, truth, equality, and freedom are always more than enough to give us hope."

The rest of the conversation was easy and honest, as they discussed her family's reaction to her announcement, her journey and the benefit and privilege of therapy. Shelley thanked him for giving her time and met Rand behind the stage. Shelley took her hand and they walked to her dressing room. There were fewer pictures on the wall than the last time she was at the show, but she didn't count them. Instead, she focused on the warmth of Rand's hand in her own and the promise of their future together.

About the Author

Jen Jensen lives in Phoenix, Arizona, with a pack of rescued senior dogs, lovely family, and friends, and spends too much time reading books.

Books Available from Bold Strokes Books

Death Overdue by David S. Pederson. Did Heath turn to murder in an alcohol induced haze to solve the problem of his blackmailer, or was it someone else who brought about a death overdue? (978-1-63555-711-4)

Entangled by Melissa Brayden. Becca Crawford is the perfect person to head up the Jade Hotel, if only the captivating owner of the local vineyard would get on board with her plan and stop badmouthing the hotel to everyone in town. (978-1-63555-709-1)

First Do No Harm by Emily Smith. Pierce and Cassidy are about to discover that when it comes to love, sometimes you have to risk it all to have it all. (978-1-63555-699-5)

Kiss Me Every Day by Dena Blake. For Wynn Jamison, wishing for a do-over with Carly Evans was a long shot, actually getting one was a game changer. (978-1-63555-551-6)

Olivia by Genevieve McCluer. In this lesbian Shakespeare adaption with vampires, Olivia is a centuries old vampire who must fight a strange figure from her past if she wants a chance at happiness. (978-1-63555-701-5)

One Woman's Treasure by Jean Copeland. Daphne's search for discarded antiques and treasures leads to an embarrassing misunderstanding, and ultimately, the opportunity for the romance of a lifetime with Nina. (978-1-63555-652-0)

Silver Ravens by Jane Fletcher. Lori has lost her girlfriend, her home, and her job. Things don't improve when she's kidnapped and taken to fairyland. (978-1-63555-631-5)

Still Not Over You by Jenny Frame, Carsen Taite, Ali Vali. Old flames die hard in these tales of a second chance at love with the ex you're still not over. Stories by award winning authors Jenny Frame, Carsen Taite, and Ali Vali. (978-1-63555-516-5)

Storm Lines by Jessica L. Webb. Devon is a psychologist who likes rules. Marley is a cop who doesn't. They don't always agree, but both fight to protect a girl immersed in a street drug ring. (978-1-63555-626-1)

The Politics of Love by Jen Jensen. Is it possible to love across the political divide in a hostile world? Conservative Shelley Whitmore and liberal Rand Thomas are about to find out. (978-1-63555-693-3)

All the Paths to You by Morgan Lee Miller. High school sweethearts Quinn Hughes and Kennedy Reed reconnect five years after they break up and realize that their chemistry is all but over. (978-1-63555-662-9)

Arrested Pleasures by Nanisi Barrett D'Arnuck. When charged with a crime she didn't commit Katherine Lowe faces the question: Which is harder, going to prison or falling in love? (978-1-63555-684-1)

Bonded Love by Renee Roman. Carpenter Blaze Carter suffers an injury that shatters her dreams, and ER nurse Trinity Greene hopes to show her that sometimes hope is worth fighting for. (978-1-63555-530-1)

Convergence by Jane C. Esther. With life as they know it on the line, can Aerin McLeary and Olivia Ando's love survive an otherworldly threat to humankind? (978-1-63555-488-5)

Coyote Blues by Karen F. Williams. Riley Dawson, psychotherapist and shape-shifter, has her world turned upside down when Fiona Bell, her one true love, returns. (978-1-63555-558-5)

Drawn by Carsen Taite. Will the clues lead Detective Claire Hanlon to the killer terrorizing Dallas, or will she merely lose her heart to person of interest, urban artist Riley Flynn? (978-1-63555-644-5)

Every Summer Day by Lee Patton. Meant to celebrate every summer day, Luke's journal instead chronicles a love affair as fast-moving and possibly as fatal as his brother's brain tumor. (978-1-63555-706-0)

Lucky by Kris Bryant. Was Serena Evans's luck really about winning the lottery, or is she about to get even luckier in love? (978-1-63555-510-3)

The Last Days of Autumn by Donna K. Ford. Autumn and Caroline question the fairness of life, the cruelty of loss, and what it means to love as they navigate the complicated minefield of relationships, grief, and life-altering illness. (978-1-63555-672-8)

Three Alarm Response by Erin Dutton. In the midst of tragedy, can these first responders find love and healing? Three stories of courage, bravery, and passion. (978-1-63555-592-9)

Veterinary Partner by Nancy Wheelton. Callie and Lauren are determined to keep their hearts safe but find that taking a chance on love is the safest option of all. (978-1-63555-666-7)

Everyday People by Louis Barr. When film star Diana Danning hires private eye Clint Steele to find her son, Clint turns to his former West Point barracks mate, and ex-buddy with benefits, Mars Hauser to lend his cyber espionage and digital black ops skills to the case. (978-1-63555-698-8)

Forging a Desire Line by Mary P. Burns. When Charley's ex-wife, Tricia, is diagnosed with inoperable cancer, the private duty nurse Tricia hires turns out to be the handsome and aloof Joanna, who ignites something inside Charley she isn't ready to face. (978-1-63555-665-0)

Love on the Night Shift by Radclyffe. Between ruling the night shift in the ER at the Rivers and raising her teenage daughter, Blaise Richilieu has all the drama she needs in her life, until a dashing young attending appears on the scene and relentlessly pursues her. (978-1-63555-668-1)

Olivia's Awakening by Ronica Black. When the daring and dangerously gorgeous Eve Monroe is hired to get Olivia Savage into shape, a fierce passion ignites, causing both to question everything they've ever known about love. (978-1-63555-613-1)

The Duchess and the Dreamer by Jenny Frame. Clementine Fitzroy has lost her faith and love of life. Can dreamer Evan Fox make her believe in life and dream again? (978-1-63555-601-8)

The Road Home by Erin Zak. Hollywood actress Gwendolyn Carter is about to discover that losing someone you love sometimes means gaining someone to fall for. (978-1-63555-633-9)

Waiting for You by Elle Spencer. When passionate past-life lovers meet again in the present day, one remembers it vividly and the other isn't so sure. (978-1-63555-635-3)

While My Heart Beats by Erin McKenzie. Can a love born amidst the horrors of the Great War survive? (978-1-63555-589-9)

Face the Music by Ali Vali. Sweet music is the last thing that happens when Nashville music producer Mason Liner, and daughter of country royalty Victoria Roddy are thrown together in an effort to save country star Sophie Roddy's career. (978-1-63555-532-5)

Flavor of the Month by Georgia Beers. What happens when baker Charlie and chef Emma realize their differing paths have led them right back to each other? (978-1-63555-616-2)

Mending Fences by Angie Williams. Rancher Bobbie Del Rey and veterinarian Grace Hammond are about to discover if heartbreaks of the past can ever truly be mended. (978-1-63555-708-4)

Silk and Leather: Lesbian Erotica with an Edge edited by Victoria Villasenor. This collection of stories by award winning authors offers fantasies as soft as silk and tough as leather. The only question is: How far will you go to make your deepest desires come true? (978-1-63555-587-5)

The Last Place You Look by Aurora Rey. Dumped by her wife and looking for anything but love, Julia Pierce retreats to her hometown, only to rediscover high school friend Taylor Winslow, who's secretly crushed on her for years. (978-1-63555-574-5)

The Mortician's Daughter by Nan Higgins. A singer on the verge of stardom discovers she must give up her dreams to live a life in service to ghosts. (978-1-63555-594-3)

The Real Thing by Laney Webber. When passion flares between actress Virginia Green and masseuse Allison McDonald, can they be sure it's the real thing? (978-1-63555-478-6)

What the Heart Remembers Most by M. Ullrich. For college sweethearts Jax Levine and Gretchen Mills, could an accident be the second chance neither knew they wanted? (978-1-63555-401-4)

White Horse Point by Andrews & Austin. Mystery writer Taylor James finds herself falling for the mysterious woman on White Horse Point who lives alone, protecting a secret she can't share about a murderer who walks among them. (978-1-63555-695-7)

Femme Tales by Anne Shade. Six women find themselves in their own real-life fairy tales when true love finds them in the most unexpected ways. (978-1-63555-657-5)

Jellicle Girl by Stevie Mikayne. One dark summer night, Beth and Jackie go out to the canoe dock. Two years later, Beth is still carrying the weight of what happened to Jackie. (978-1-63555-691-9)

Le Berceau by Julius Eks. If only Ben could tear his heart in two, then he wouldn't have to choose between the love of his life and the most beautiful boy he has ever seen. (978-1-63555-688-9)

My Date with a Wendigo by Genevieve McCluer. Elizabeth Rosseau finds her long lost love and the secret community of fiends she's now a part of. (978-1-63555-679-7)

On the Run by Charlotte Greene. Even when they're cute blondes, it's stupid to pick up hitchhikers, especially when they've just broken out of prison, but doing so is about to change Gwen's life forever. (978-1-63555-682-7)

Perfect Timing by Dena Blake. The choice between love and family has never been so difficult, and Lynn's and Maggie's different visions of the future may end their romance before it's begun. (978-1-63555-466-3)

The Mail Order Bride by R Kent. When a mail order bride is thrust on Austin, he must choose between the bride he never wanted or the dream he lives for. (978-1-63555-678-0)

Through Love's Eyes by C.A. Popovich. When fate reunites Brittany Yardin and Amy Jansons, can they move beyond the pain of their past to find love? (978-1-63555-629-2)

To the Moon and Back by Melissa Brayden. Film actress Carly Daniel thinks that stage work is boring and unexciting, but when she accepts a lead role in a new play, stage manager Lauren Prescott tests both her heart and her ability to share the limelight. (978-1-63555-618-6)

Tokyo Love by Diana Jean. When Kathleen Schmitt is given the opportunity to be on the cutting edge of AI technology, she never thought a failed robotic love companion would bring her closer to her neighbor, Yuriko Velucci, and finding love in unexpected places. (978-1-63555-681-0)